UNCLE SHAWN AND BILL

UNCLE SHAWN AND BILL

AND THE GREAT BIG PURPLE UNDERWATER UNDERPANTS ADVENTURE

A. L. KENNEDY

ILLUSTRATED BY GEMMA CORRELL

WALKER
BOOKS

First published 2020 by Walker Books Ltd
87 Vauxhall Walk, London SE11 5HJ

This edition published in 2021

2 4 6 8 10 9 7 5 3 1

Text © 2020 A. L. Kennedy • Illustrations © 2020 Gemma Correll

The right of A. L. Kennedy and Gemma Correll to be identified as author and illustrator respectively of this work has been asserted by them in accordance with the Copyright, Designs and Patents Act 1988

This book has been typeset in Sabon and Gemma Correll Regular

Printed and bound in Great Britain by CPI Group (UK) Ltd, Croydon CR0 4YY

British Library Cataloguing in Publication Data: a catalogue record for this book is available from the British Library

ISBN 978-1-4063-9881-6

www.walker.co.uk

For Honor, Xavier and V.D.B.

INNOCENT SCONES

SECTION ONE

In which there are some innocent scones and some excited raindrops and all our friends on Uncle Shawn's llama farm are definitely not expecting their biggest adventure yet...

All over the world a Particularly Purple Problem was happening. It was just the sort of thing that would have made Uncle Shawn rub his long, wiggly fingers in his long, wiggly hair to make his long, wiggly brain start thinking up ideas that would fix any problem (and rescue anyone who needed rescuing). But Uncle Shawn was sitting in his favourite chair, eating an apple and looking at excited raindrops chasing each other down his window. He didn't know anything about the Particularly Purple Problem.

The Particularly Purple Problem would have frizzled Badger Bill's whiskers with fright. But Bill had just finished baking marmalade scones in Uncle Shawn's farmhouse and hadn't heard anything about Purpleness or Problems.

The Particularly Purple Problem would have worried Guinevere and Carlos Llama, but they were inside their cosy llama barn on Uncle Shawn's farm, playing snap. Carlos had just yelled "Snap!" even though he only had a card showing an orangutan wearing a hat. Guinevere had just put down a card showing a tiger making rice pudding – and that isn't the same at all. Guinevere was too busy shouting, "You great big smelly and cheating llama!" to look out for a Particularly Purple Problem.

Ginalolobrigida Llama was busy reading a book

STACK
ORANGUTAN WEARING A HAT
GER MAKING CE PUDDING

about the incredibly clever and handsome llama athlete Alfonso Aparador. Alfonso could make Brazilian brown bats drop out of the sky just by grinning at them with his beautiful teeth or reciting his fabulous poems. He could sing like a sack full of nightingales (never put nightingales in sacks – they don't like it), and jaguars he met in the Peruvian forests would never try to eat him. In fact, they would purr and gently lick his ears. Ginalolobrigida thought Alfonso sounded almost good enough to be her boyfriend, as long as he washed the puma

ALFONSO APARADOR

IS HE THE PERFECT LLAMA?

Olympic Champ

opera singer

Award Winning CHEF

Jaguar Therapist

- IS THERE NOTHING HE CAN'T DO? WHAT IS THE TRUTH ABOUT ALFONSO? Is he more perfect than we already thought.....?!

spit out of his ears. Even if she had known about the Particularly Purple Problem, it would have seemed much less interesting than Alfonso.

Of course, Brian Llama was already too worried to have any room for more worry in his poor, hot llama head. He worried that his hooves might be stolen while he was asleep. He worried that if he stayed awake all night guarding his hooves he might get so tired he wouldn't notice big holes in the ground and would fall into them. There weren't any big holes in the ground near Uncle Shawn's farm, but that just made Brian worry he couldn't practise falling into them and then climbing back out.

Claude the spider was bouncing and swinging from the rafters in Brian's barn and hanging raindrops from his web to make nice sparkling shapes for Brian. But Brian sighed, "Oh, Señor Claude spider, sir, I wish I had some other llamas in my barn to keep me company. No one will have sleepovers with me because I make too much noise at night counting my hooves to check I still have four... You, Señor Claude, are very brave, but much smaller than a hoof thief... Or an ear thief... Or an eyebrow thief... Oh, emergencia, there are so many parts of me that someone could steal..."

Brian looked so worried that Claude gave him

the Peruvian hat made out of spiderwebs (with pompoms) which was supposed to be saved for a birthday surprise. Brian and Claude were too busy to know about the Particularly Purple Problem.

Sam and Sky were waiting in the farmhouse kitchen, ready to eat marmalade scones as soon as Bill said they were cool enough. They were having a competition to see which one of them had the loudest tummy rumbles. Sky won. But the Particularly Purple Problem was bigger than any tummy rumble.

Maybe the Particularly Purple Problem was going to be fun and friendly. Or maybe it was so terrible that all our friends would have to face dreadful adventures and strange journeys and gigantunormous nightmares! And maybe the Most Terrible Human on Earth was committing his worst crimes ever! Purple Crimes!

Oh, no!

Emergencia! 🐾

UNDER-PANTS

SECTION TWO

In which there are underpants. And someone even more wicked than Montague Nipfinger, the nastiest school caretaker in Aberdeen (who is deeply nasty).

While Uncle Shawn was in Scotland getting scone crumbs in his hair, in London's biggest law courts a master criminal was on trial. And there were no scones allowed.

Wickedest human in the world, Sylvester Pearlyclaws, was standing in the dock between two policemen and saying, "Can you repeat the charges, your honourable worshipness?" He was using his sneakiest voice because he wanted to be let off with a warning so that he could go home and eat toast and plan more wickedness.

He was wearing his least frightening shirt – to help him look less guilty – but his enormous boots, prison-issue false teeth and false nose were still quite scary. He blamed Uncle Shawn for the shoes and teeth – and the nose! Uncle Shawn was the happiest person in the world and Pearlyclaws was allergic to happiness, so Pearlyclaws' only hobby was trying to destroy Uncle Shawn. The first time Pearlyclaws tried to squash Uncle Shawn's happiness, Pearlyclaws had squeezed his own teeth so hard they exploded. Now his grey prison teeth made everything – even toffee – taste of cabbage, and that was Uncle Shawn's fault!

The second time Pearlyclaws tried to make Uncle Shawn miserable, Pearlyclaws' nose had been swooshed right off by a comet. His prison-issue false nose didn't fit and whistled when he got out of breath. That was Uncle Shawn's fault, too!

Pearlyclaws' feet – which had been his pride and joy – had been squashed flat by the same comet. This morning – and every morning – he had to fold his feet up like angry, pink pancakes and push them into his unhappy socks. (You have to be extra-wicked to make your own socks unhappy.) When he squeezed his squishy socks into the biggest possible size of prison boots, this was Uncle Shawn's fault too!

Now Pearlyclaws smiled with his scary prison teeth and tried to look as free from crime and wicked- ness as a newly-baked

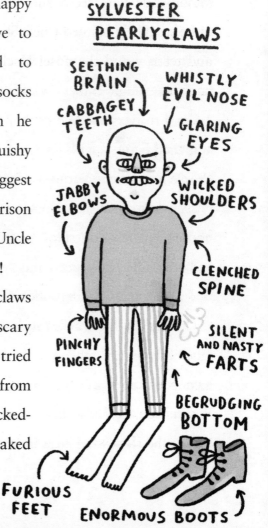

SYLVESTER PEARLYCLAWS

SEETHING BRAIN

WHISTLY EVIL NOSE

CABBAGEY TEETH

GLARING EYES

JABBY ELBOWS

WICKED SHOULDERS

CLENCHED SPINE

PINCHY FINGERS

SILENT AND NASTY FARTS

BEGRUDGING BOTTOM

FURIOUS FEET

ENORMOUS BOOTS

scone. (Scones are almost never wicked.) But he was wicked – as wicked as someone cancelling your summer holiday or shouting at kittens.

As Judge Norris looked at Pearlyclaws' grin, his wig started itching. Usually Judge Norris loved his wig. When he was a little boy he had always wanted to wear one of the special great big curly wigs that judges put on while they're at work to make sure everyone knows they are in charge. He had tried being a milkman and a zoo keeper, but people had laughed at him when he wore a great big, curly judge's wig to leave yoghurt and milk bottles on their doorsteps, or to feed giraffes. So he had studied very hard and become a judge.

In his loudest voice, Judge Norris announced, "Sylvester Wilberforce Humbertly Pearlyclaws (also known as Sylvester T. Pearlyclaws), you have been found guilty of stealing all the wool in Wales. You have also been found guilty of stealing all the clockwork toys in England."

He continued, "Sylvester Wilberforce Humbertly Pearlyclaws, Scotland is also very cross with you because you have stolen all of their clockwork toys. Once I have sentenced you to for ever in prison, my Scottish friend Judge Cox will want to do the same."

Then Judge Norris shouted, "And right now I am charging you with prodding Constable Nimmo so hard in the ribs using your pointy finger that he squeaked and I am finding you very, very guilty! BECAUSE I HAVE JUST SEEN YOU DO IT! YOU ARE EXTREMELY WICKED ALL OVER AND YOU HAVE MADE POOR CONSTABLE NIMMO CRY!"

While Constable Nimmo sniffled bravely and his friend Constable Barnard gave him a peppermint to cheer him up, Pearlyclaws lied in his weaseliest voice, "But I have never done anything wicked in my life." He was just about to lie some more when—

FF**BOO**MFF!

A deep-purple cloud suddenly burst out all around Pearlyclaws' bottom and his trousers split apart.

"Eeek!" yelled the two constables.

"Ook!" yelled Judge Norris and then, "Keep calm everyone! I am being very calm! I am not afraid at all! Judges have special training to deal with purple bottom clouds!"

Only then—

FF**BOO**MFF!

Judge Norris was suddenly surrounded by a huge cloud of purple smoke and felt his trousers get very draughty.

"I'm not scared, either!" squeaked Constable Nimmo.

"Nor me!" squawked Constable Barnard.

And, as soon as they did...

FF**BOO**MFF!
FF**BOO**MFF!

There was a Particularly Purple Problem in the whole courtroom. A Particularly Purple Pant Problem!

In the confusion, Sylvester Pearlyclaws giggled – which sounded like frog farts in a bath – and slipped

out of his handcuffs. His mother had taught him how to do this when he was six, just before she taught him 57 ways to make strangers cry and how to tie his laces.

"We're not afraid!" shouted all the people in the jury. This was probably a mistake because…

FF**BOO**MFF! FF**BOO**MFF!
FF**BOO**MFF! FF**BOO**MFF!
FF**BOO**MFF! FF**BOO**MFF!
FF**BOO**MFF! FF**BOO**MFF!
FF**BOO**MFF! FF**BOO**MFF!

Purple clouds exploded from their bottoms, even though they were sitting down. In fact, two of them were pushed to their feet by the force of purpleness whooshing out of their skirts.

The constables guarding Pearlyclaws were blinded by the purple powdery smoke and busy using their hats to cover the gaps that had been blown in their trousers. They couldn't see Pearlyclaws taking off his boots and unfolding his feet until they were spread out on the floor like two big angry, cheesy omelettes. This meant his huge, flat feet didn't sound like feet any more – they sounded like two big, flat flounder fish flapping over the floorboards. While the jury and the ushers and everyone in the court coughed and saw nothing but purple, nobody had time to wonder why they could hear two big, flat flounder fish flipping and flapping away in a perfectly dry court, far from the sea in the middle of London.

The Particularly Purple Problem had given the world's worst criminal the perfect chance to escape! Almost as if he had a Particularly Purple Plan!

And while he slop-slapped along London's busy streets, Pearlyclaws growled, "I will get you, Uncle Shawn. I will get you and I will make you cry and – Ooya! Ouchy! Ouchy! Look where you're going!" His feet were so enormous it was impossible for people to avoid treading on them. He wanted to vow revenge on Uncle Shawn all the way to the secret lair he kept by the River Thames, but he kept having to say, "Oo-ya!" instead when people squashed his already-squished feet. Then a taxi driver parked on his left foot for ten minutes.

All this made him angrier than cats wearing buttered mittens trying to climb trees, angrier than Lesser Spotted Furious Lizards whose birthday presents have been lost in the post, angrier than Empress Matilda of Trinsylmania who was always so furious with her subjects that eventually they all ran away, having rolled up the whole country and taken it with them.

EMPRESS MATILDA OF TRINSYLMANIA

They rolled it out flat again, lifted up Belgium while everyone was asleep and hid their country underneath. That is why you have never heard of Trinsylmania.

The angrier Pearlyclaws got, the more out of breath he got, so that his nose whistled – *ffeeep, ffeeep* – wherever he went.

As Pearlyclaws flapped and flooped along the muddy shore of the Thames, the river breezes chilled his evil bottom through the split in his trousers. And he muttered, "I'll catch you Uncle Shawn and – *ffeeep, ffeeep* – I'll flatten you Uncle Shawn! – *ffeeep, ffeeep* – I'll fillet you! I'll fry you and – *ffeeep, ffeeep* – eat you up with chips!"

Oh no!

Emergencia! 🐾

EXPLODING UNDER-PANTS

SECTION THREE

In which there are more powdered pants!
We'll have to hope Uncle Shawn finds out
what's wrong before everyone ends up feeling
very draughty around their bottoms...

Meanwhile, in the House of Commons (where Britain's politicians make speeches at each other and eat cake) a very famous MP stood up to make what he hoped would be his best speech ever.

He waited for everyone to be quiet. Then he announced, "I am magnificent! Everything I do is magnificent! You can trust me!"

Everyone who agreed with him waved their

hands and shouted, "Yes! You are wonderful! And so are we!" Everyone who disagreed shouted, "Boo! No! We are wonderful!" But then—

FFBOOMFF!

Hundreds of expensive underpants burst all over the expensive green leather benches that MPs sit on. Huge purple clouds leaped up into the air as high as badgers dancing the Dance of Badger Delight. All the MPs had to go home to fetch new skirts and trousers.

And meanwhile, up in Pandrumdroochit village, Mrs McWoollyguggle was wheeling her brand new pram along the high street. Peering out from the pram was her brand new baby Fergus McWoollyguggle. Passing the sweet shop, she met the headmaster of Pandrumdroochit School, Mr Flowers. He had been looking at children since nine o'clock in the morning and didn't really want to see another young face until tomorrow – especially not a baby's. But Mrs McWoollyguggle insisted that

Mr Flowers look at her son's quite hairy head and quite large ears and quite wriggly nose – along with the lumpy green hat that she had knitted for him with F-E-R-G-U-S spelled out in tiny red bobbles. Fergus looked a bit like a little rabbit, staring out from under a very infectious cabbage.

"Ah!" Mr Flowers couldn't help screaming. But then he remembered you're supposed to be polite about other people's babies. He told Mrs McWoollyguggle, "How lovely that, um … small person is." But then—

FFBOOMFF!

A huge purple cloud whooshed out around Mr Flowers and the pram and Fergus and Mrs McWoollyguggle. And that was the end of the headmaster's favourite trousers and his favourite underpants.

And in Singapore a lady told her husband that his new hat made him look handsome and then—

FFBOOMFF!

A cloud of powdery purple everywhere and no more underpants!

And in Brisbane Nancy Minden told Patsy Minden, "I love that dress – it doesn't make you look like a sad horse trying to eat a tablecloth." And then—

FFBOOMFF!

More purple! More powdered underpants!

And in Munich's biggest and nicest cake shop, Ehrhard T. Adrian Hoffman told his Auntie Mitzi, "No it's all right, I don't want any cake." And then—

EHRHARD T. ADRIAN HOFFMAN

AUNTIE MITZI

FFBOOMFF!

A purple cloud of used-to-be-underpants made Ehrhard split his lederhosen. (He didn't mind his lederhosen being ruined, because he only wore them to please his Auntie Mitzi. They were too small and made his knees numb.)

In Liverpool and Lima – **FFBOOMFF!**

In Riga – **FFBOOMFF!**

In Riyadh – **FFBOOMFF!**

In Baghdad – **FFBOOMFF!**

In every country on Earth – except Trinsylmania because it was hidden under Belgium – **FFBOOMFF!** – the Particularly Purple Problem was happening!

As the days passed, purple clouds drifted everywhere, like the smell of egg sandwiches somebody cruel has kept in a hot box for a week. Forecasters began to add a new kind of weather to their forecasts – Purple.

PURPLE HEN →

BURP!

SECTION FOUR

In which there are beaks, bottoms and feathers. And a Particularly Purple Problem Adventure is on the way! Or maybe a Great Big Purple Underpants Adventure!

A week after the Particularly Purple Problem started, Badger Bill was watching the sunrise from the farmhouse veranda, sitting in his little badger rocking chair. All the llamas were still asleep and dreaming. Sam and Sky were dreaming in their cosy beds and cosy pyjamas. And Uncle Shawn was dreaming in his really long bed and his really long pyjamas.

The farmhouse was still perfectly tidy with no

llama fur, or llama spit, or fingerprints, or jam, or hoof prints anywhere. This made Bill smile, because he was a very neat badger. As soon as everyone woke up the place would look as if it had been loaded into a cement mixer full of hair, mud, marmalade, custard and hooves, so Bill was making the most of the peace. Bill was wearing his favourite big hat which he thought made him look like a pirate. Everyone else thought it made him look like a small, plump badger wearing a big hat, but they were too polite to say so.

Bill sighed happily. "Mmmm. Everywhere is neat and quiet." He looked over the Pandrumdroochit Hills. "The sky seems a bit … purple… Hmmm… I wonder if there is anything wrong… No, I'm sure everything is fine. And thank goodness Mr Pearlyclaws is safely locked away in prison. He's exactly the kind of wicked person who would make the sky purple just to upset everyone."

CONTENT BADGER

OMINOUS PURPLE SKY

SORT-OF-BUT-NOT-REALLY PIRATE HAT

He rocked his rocking chair back and forth, closed his eyes and hummed his latest favourite tune, Beautiful Badger Boogie Blues. "Although..." He grinned. "Maybe a teeny tiny adventure might be fun. We haven't had one for ages and adventures with Uncle Shawn are the best kind of adventures you can have."

Then he heard an odd noise coming closer across the fields. It sounded like 400 purple hens burping.

FFBOOMFF! FFBOOMFF!

The noise was getting louder...

FFBOOMFF!

And nearer...

FFBOOMFF!

Until it was much too near altogether.

FFBOOMFF!

FFBOOMFF!

Bill's sensitive badger nose could smell dusty llama fur and fresh llama spit and Ginalolobrigida Llama's delicious perfume Moyobamba Moonlight (Orchid Flavour) and something else he had never smelled before that seemed a bit ... purple.

"You are the world's most ignorant, flea-bitten, cheating-at-snap-and-everything-else   llama!   I hate you!"

FFBOOMFF!

Poor Bill opened his eyes just in time to see a huge purple cloud with Guinevere's voice inside it.

Then Carlos's voice shouted, "I hate you! I

have always hated you! Since before I was born!"

Only then—

FFBOOMFF!

Then Bill heard Ginalolobrigida's most llama-ladylike voice: "Well, I am sure this happens all the time to foolish llamas who won't use moisturiser. I myself will never be covered in purpleness which does not match my Gorgeous Green Goddess eyeshadow." Then—

FFBOOMFF!

The cloud of purple grew even more massive.

Bill's long stripy nose was full of purpleness by now and he had no idea why three of his llama friends seemed to be inside a huge cloud. "My goodness! What on earth is happening?!"

Then the farmhouse door banged open and two child-shaped clouds of purple rushed out, shouting at each other.

"I did not pinch you!" said Sky's voice from inside her patch of purple.

FFBOOMFF!

"Yes, you did!" said Sam's voice from inside his patch of purple. "Now you're not invisible I can always see you when you pinch me!"

"Well, you wore my favourite sweater and made a hole in the sleeve!"

"That was moths!"

FFBOOMFF!

"Oooohhh, what is happening please Mr Bill, please and thank you!" shouted Brian Llama's voice from inside the thicker and thicker

purpleness. "Ooooohh, what if someone steals my hooves while I can't see them?! Maybe they are stealing them right now! *Emergenciaaaaaaa…!*"

Bill could hear Brian's hooves clopping round and round in frightened circles, still attached to Brian and somewhere inside the high, thick bank of purpleness.

Just then, Uncle Shawn opened his bedroom window, stuck out his head and called down, "Good morning Bill! Good morning everybody! What a wonderful day – a bit too purple, though… Hmmm…"

Just hearing Uncle Shawn's voice made Bill feel his fur relax and his ears get calmer. Uncle Shawn always knew what to do.

Uncle Shawn called, "Bill, where would you go to find out the weight of a whale?"

Bill smiled and shouted back, "You take it to a Whale Way Station, Uncle Shawn!"

"Of course you do!" Uncle Shawn laughed and then whistled a very complicated whistle Bill had never heard before: "*Pooteetootletweetoot!*"

"I think we need less purpley powdery smoke out there," said Uncle Shawn, shaking his head because some purple had got inside his ears and was tickling his thinking. "Otherwise we won't be able to see our own breakfasts.

UNCLE SHAWN'S BRAIN

Jokes for Bill · Other jokes · Inspiration · Dance moves · Day dreams · Hope · Kindness · Ideas for flying machines · Recipes · Guesses

PURPLE TICKLING HIS THINKING

Hmmm... I do hope there is nothing wrong with the Living Fish Tree." And he whistled again, "*Pooteetootletweetoot!* I think we need some special help."

"The Living Fish Tree?" said Bill. "I've never heard a joke about a Living Fish Tree."

"Oh, she would be most upset if you called her a joke," said Uncle Shawn.

"Do we need an adventure?" shouted Sam from inside the purple cloud.

"Yes, do we?" shouted Sky.

"Hmmm... Well, a Living Fish Tree adventure might be extremely dangerous and difficult." Uncle Shawn grinned down at Bill. "Or it might be fun. If we don't all end up tickled in terrible traps, or poked with prickly prods, or flung into floomy floods..."

"Waaaaaah!" yelled Brian's voice from the cloud. "I don't want to be flung, please and thank you!"

Carlos shouted out, "We would save you, Brian!"

"Oh, I am sure we will always save each other, because we are friends and that's what friends do..." Uncle Shawn winked at Bill. "But I think there might be a gigantunormous adventure on

the way and – goodness me – we have no plan...
Not even a little bit of one."

Then he winked one of his
biggest winks, as if a Purple
Adventure With No Plan
would be the very best thing
to do with your best friend.
Bill felt much less scared and
much more excited.

"Help is on the way!" Uncle Shawn smiled. "I
have whistled the Come and Help Call! Look, it's
working already!"

Birds of every kind began to arrive at the farmhouse. Patient owls and excited sparrows, tiny
wrens and robins and huge buzzards and golden
eagles all swirled about overhead, flapping as hard
as they could. After only a few feathery minutes
the purple had been waved and whooshed away
by the birds' wings. Everyone could see everybody again.

BELGIAN
COUGHING
OWL

SNAKE-
EATING
DOOM BUZZARD

GREY CARDIGAN
CREEPER

As the birds settled down to perch on the bushes and trees and even the llamas, Uncle Shawn rushed down the farmhouse stairs and out onto the veranda. He gave his best friend Bill a good morning hug. "I ran down the stairs in my pyjamas, Bill."

"That's a funny place to have stairs." Bill giggled.

Uncle Shawn laughed and crumbled the biscuits he always kept in his pyjama pockets into tiny pieces, which he threw in handfuls up into the air for the little birds to eat. He was always

STINK WINGED BLART BIRD

YELLOW COCKAMAMIE

LESSER SARCASTIC BLUEBIRD

HORNED BISCUIT FINCHES

very kind to the birds he met and fed them and helped them find their lost babies, or gave them small tufts of his wibbly hair they could use to line their nests. This was why they had taught him many of their most useful whistles.

"*Stwee-ee! Stwee-ee!*" called a very tall golden eagle landing right next to Brian. She stared at him with her stern eyes, while her knife-sharp beak flashed in the sunshine.

Brian jumped. "Whoo-aa! Please do not eat me, Señora Big Eagle! I am too scared to taste nice!"

Uncle Shawn leaned over and stroked Brian's ears. "She is just asking for a dish of water to drink, because she flew a long way very fast to get here. And the starlings would like some cheese and the blackbirds need some stale scones and can we make some fish paste sandwiches for the seagulls, Bill?"

"AA-KEEYEE-KWA-KWA-KWA!" yelled a big herring gull. (Gulls have to yell over the high winds that blow across oceans next to cliffs. They also just enjoy yelling.)

Uncle Shawn bent his bony knees and nodded in a herring gull kind of way. "This is Logan Herring Gull, Bill. And he would like a banana and sardine sundae."

Soon the farmhouse kitchen was full of birds eating, birds reading comics, birds perching and hopping and pecking everywhere you looked.

Outside on the veranda, Uncle Shawn was squawking sad and serious squawks with a wise

BIRD DESSERTS

BANANA AND SARDINE SUNDAE

FLOOR CHIPS

WEEK OLD PIZZA

EARTHWORM AND COCKROACH SURPRISE

and elderly seagull and hooting sad and serious hoots with an even more wise and elderly owl and he was rubbing his nose against the big, deadly beak of an osprey and nodding.

Then Uncle Shawn and the seagull and the owl and the osprey all turned to study the ever-more-purple patches that were drifting across many far-away bits of the sky. Bill noticed them all shaking their heads as if there really was a Particularly Purple Problem – and it was spreading...

SECTION FIVE

In which Pearlyclaws is up to something...
And there are some nice rats.

Pearlyclaws sat on his wet, smelly chair in his wet, smelly Supervillain Lair that was really just a few rooms dug out in the side of a large sewer pipe. Sometimes he stared for hours and hours at a huge wall made up of television screens. The screens showed all kinds of peculiar pictures. On one there were flying jam sandwiches and on another pirates were swinging from rigging in stormy seas and singing pirate songs. There were lots of llamas, too – llamas dancing and juggling and cooking and walking on tightropes and steering barges across Lake Titicaca while wearing startling green eyeshadow.

Sometimes he stared at a tall jar he kept in a corner, labelled: **PURPLONIUM!**

Inside the jar purplonium wriggled and climbed the glass as if it was at least a little bit alive. Whenever it climbed high enough to push the lid off the jar, Pearlyclaws would shout, "Sit!" Then it would go back to lying at the bottom of the jar.

Pearlyclaws owned all the purplonium in the world. Sometimes he would lift out bits of glowing purplonium with his thick safety gloves and look at it lovingly through his eye-defence goggles. Tiny lumps of it would scamper up and down his fingers and seem to wink at him wickedly, as if purplonium was the most evil substance on Earth. Which it was!!!

In case you don't know, purplonium is the most evil substance in the whole wide universe. It was made by mistake centuries ago and has been getting more evil ever since.

Katie and Bernard Pinktail didn't care about purplonium. They were the two sewer rats who

Katie &
Bernard
Pinktail

looked after the lair while Pearlyclaws was away being wicked. They were in charge of cleaning and shopping and checking all the watertight doors and valves that kept the Thames from coming in and washing everything away.

The rats didn't like Pearlyclaws' monitor screens, because they always showed silly things instead of romantic dramas with handsome singing rats. They didn't like Pearlyclaws, either – he pulled their tender pink tails and called them names.

"Just because we are rats and live in a sewer that doesn't mean we don't have feelings," Bernard whispered to his wife, hoping that Pearlyclaws wouldn't hear him.

"I know, dearest. I was hoping he'd be sent to prison for a long time and then we could have redecorated his Sitting Room of Evil and got some nice armchairs down here," whispered Katie.

They rubbed noses gently and then scampered away along the main sewer pipe, treading on soft, smelly, squelchy things that we won't think about – which they didn't mind at all, because of being sewer rats. They had caught the scent of some really nice rotting broccoli in Mayfair and wanted to get the best bits for their tea.

Pearlyclaws' Sitting Room of Evil only had one big leather chair (with threatening arms), because no one was evil enough to sit there except him. His Supervillain Lair also had a Dungeon of Despair. He planned to lock Uncle Shawn up in it, along with all his friends. At the moment, hidden in the dungeon were pieces of the clockwork toys Pearlyclaws had stolen. It looked as if he was building something. Whatever he built probably wouldn't be a cuddle dispenser, or musical boxes to cheer up old anacondas who live alone.

When being so nasty had made him tired, Pearlyclaws slept in his damp, smelly bed in his slimy Bedroom of Nastiness. His lair also had a very small Bathroom of Horror and a Kitchenette of Wickedness, where he never cooked anything except toast which tasted just as bad as you can imagine toast would if you made it in a sewer and were the most evil man alive.

SMELLY OOZE

DRIPS OF NASTINESS

BATHROOM OF HORROR

DAMP-PROOF JARS

Teeth   Noses   Toe Nails

COLD SLIMY TOOTH-BRUSH

Nose Polish

SITTING ROOM OF EVIL

ITCHY BLANKET

PEARLY CLAWS SHOCKS POPE

PEARLY CLAWS FRIGHTENS WHALES

FRAMED HEAD-LINES

PEARLY CLAWS FRIGHTENS WALES

RAT ACCESS HOLE

DUNGEON

DUNG BEETLES

POO PILE

GLOWING PURPLONIUM

SEWER PIPE

As Pearlyclaws buttered his toast, or took spoonfuls of glowing purplonium dust and scattered it over the cogs and springs he had stolen from so many clockwork toys, his false nose whistled with fury – *ffeeep, ffeeep*. His false teeth clenched and he muttered under his breath, "I will get you, Uncle Shawn. And I will get all of your friends. I will get you more got than getting gets gotted!"

And the purplonium shone and the clockwork pieces shivered and shuddered, almost as if they were coming to life. Pearlyclaws was building something nasty!

Oh no!

Emergencia! 🐾

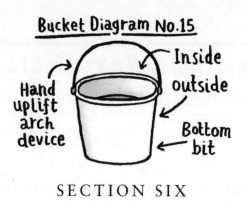

Bucket Diagram No.15

Inside

Hand
uplift
arch
device

outside

Bottom
bit

SECTION SIX

In which lots of creatures are having
Particularly Purple Problems.

Meanwhile, in Pandrumdroochit village, the Pandrumdroochit Pudding Day Planning Committee was holding a meeting. Really, there wasn't much need for planning. Pudding Day was held on the thirteenth Thursday of the year. Everyone in the village made as many different puddings as they could and then ate them, or swapped them with neighbours, or gave them to strangers, or took them to Pandrumdroochit Community Hall for the Midnight Pudding

ARE YOU - WEAK? FEEBLE? BULLIED BY KITTENS?

STRIKE BACK WITH PUDDING SELF DEFENCE

PSD CAN HELP YOU...

- BAFFLE YOUR ENEMIES WITH CUSTARD
- PREVENT BANK ROBBERIES USING ECLAIRS*
- WIN ANY ARGUMENT WITH
  ICE CREAM AND SPRINKLES

* USE OF ECLAIRS FOR ADVANCED STUDENTS ONLY

Celebration. There were prizes for the tastiest pudding and the prettiest pudding, pudding self-defence classes and – of course – pudding eating. This always happened. Still, the committee members liked to meet up every month, just to talk about puddings and look at pudding pictures.

Angus MacLeod was explaining how celebrity pudding chef Felicity Mumbleduck cooked chocolate pudding in buckets at the edge of volcanoes. Although this could have been exciting, Angus had spent 45 minutes describing her buckets and no minutes describing her leaping about in flame-proof boots to avoid big spurts of white-hot lava, or dodging flying lumps of boiling rock. This all made Harry Simms yawn.

"Am I boring you?" asked Angus, looking up from Bucket Diagram Number 15 (the one with the very good view of the handle).

"No. Not at all." But as soon as Harry said this…

I think you can guess…

FFBOOMFF!

Harry Simms disappeared in a huge puff of purple smoke and his bottom got chilly.

While he was shouting, "Oh, my underpants!" Angus was shouting, "There's no need to throw smoke bombs! You said you liked my lectures!"

Everyone around the table shouted, "No, no. We love bucket lectures!" This was a nice thing to say, but it wasn't exactly true. And so…

FF**BOO**MFF!
FF**BOO**MFF!
FF**BOO**MFF!

All around the committee table whooshes and pushes of purple smoke blew upwards and outwards and the hems of kilts flew up into the air and underpants vanished!

The Pandrumdroochit Pudding Day Planning Committee had never known anything like it. And while they stared into the purplish air all around them, they wondered if they would have to invent a new prize – for Purple Puddings.

Meanwhile, in the rest of the world, aeroplane pilots were refusing to fly because the new purple clouds everywhere were making it hard to see. Purple rain was starting to fall and was making lakes and rivers taste purple. Plants were starting to droop because the purple was stopping them from getting enough sunshine. And everywhere

– apart from Trinsylmania – people's underpants were disappearing.

Almost the only people in the world who were happy were underpants makers. They had never been as busy in their whole lives. They would run up and down inside their underpants workshops, laughing and yelling, "It's as if everybody has grown an extra bottom! Or two! Or three! Hooray!"

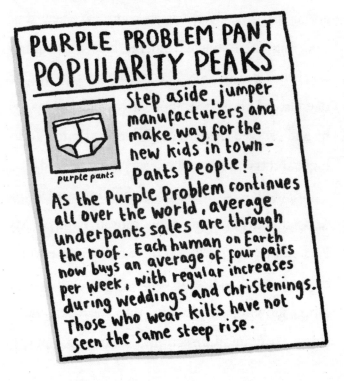

PURPLE PROBLEM PANT POPULARITY PEAKS

purple pants

Step aside, jumper manufacturers and make way for the new kids in town – Pants People!

As the Purple Problem continues all over the world, average underpants sales are through the roof. Each human on Earth now buys an average of four pairs per week, with regular increases during weddings and christenings. Those who wear kilts have not seen the same steep rise.

And meanwhile, Pearlyclaws was standing in the mud at the edge of the Thames, close to the big sewer pipe where his secret lair was hidden in the slithery and stinky darkness.

Sitting behind him on a nice sandy dry patch (they didn't like to get their tender tails muddy) were Katie and Bernard Pinktail, the sewer rats. They would rather have been in their own little corner of the sewer, eating some excellent stale cake they had stolen from the bins of a luxury hotel, but Pearlyclaws liked boasting and had no one else he could tell about his wicked plans, so he had ordered them to sit and look at him admiringly and try to remember everything he said.

"Behold!" he announced, holding a seething mass of purplonium in his gloved hands. "My Particularly Purple Plot is the worst plot the world has ever seen!" Then he threw the wriggling, giggling, glowing purplonium into the river and it swam away in all directions, leaving little purple trails. Pearlyclaws watched it and tried to laugh an evil laugh. Then he went on about being a genius, but his ill-fitting prison nose made *ffeeep, ffeeep* noises at the same time, so he just sounded as if he was arguing with a budgie.

Katie whispered to her husband, "If I closed my eyes, I would think his nose noise was a pair of rusty roller skates, complaining while they roll down a hill."

Bernard sniggered. "Or an angry alarm clock."

ANGRY ALARM CLOCK

"All alarm clocks are angry – that's why they shout so much when you want to keep on sleeping," Katie muttered.

"Would you mind speaking up a bit – we can't hear you over your nose," said Bernard Pinktail.

This annoyed Pearlyclaws, so his nose *ffeeeped* even more loudly than usual. "You ridiculous vermin! *Ffeeep, ffeeep!* I don't know why I don't stamp on your – *ffeeep, ffeeep!* – tails until I am tired!"

"Because it would hurt your floppy rolled-up feet, you big bully," whispered Katie, while both rats tried to look very respectful.

Pearlyclaws stared at them hard, then continued, "Every time I drop purplonium into the river, it spreads and spreads all through the water and eventually all over – *ffeeep, ffeeep* – the world! Purplonium will infect the rain and the lakes and lochs – *ffeeep, ffeeep* – and every time anyone on Earth drinks anything – *ffeeep, ffeeep* – they will be drinking purplonium, too. The more purplonium they drink the more I can control them. I can already see every single one of their dreams on my monitors!"

"Well, why would you bother with that?" Katie Pinktail murmured to her chuckling husband.

"I dreamed all my paws were bright orange last night. Why anyone would want to watch that, I can't imagine…" replied Bernard Pinktail.

"I can – *ffeeep, ffeeep* – HEAR YOU!!!" screamed Pearlyclaws. "I am surrounded by idiots!"

"We're not surrounding you – we're behind you."

"If you don't shut up, I will pull your ears off and use them as waistcoat buttons."

This was so nasty it made the rats go quiet and put their paws over their ears.

Pearlyclaws went on, "If I can see your dreams, I can turn them into nightmares! And I can make all your nightmares come true! ALL OVER THE WORLD I WILL – *ffeeep, ffeeep* – MAKE SURE  THERE IS AT LEAST ONE MONSTER – *ffeeep, ffeeep* – UNDER EVERY CHILD'S BED!!! AND **TWO MONSTERS AT THE WEEKENDS!!!!!**"

"That's just silly," murmured Bernard. "The monster would eat all the crumbs under the beds and then what would the children nibble if they got hungry in the night?"

"And what about the children with no beds?" Katie said.

"I WILL PROVIDE – *ffeeep, ffeeep* – A BED FOR EVERY CHILD!!" Then Pearlyclaws realised this would be a nice thing to do, so then he had to yell even more loudly, **"I WILL MAKE SURE THE BEDS ARE LUMPY!"**

The rats just shook their heads and scampered away over the mud on their clever paws. When Pearlyclaws was this angry they knew he would definitely try to pull their tails and nobody likes having their tail pulled – especially by a *ffeeeping* supervillain.

Pearlyclaws didn't notice they had gone. He just stared at the lapping water of the Thames and the peculiar purple stains spreading out across it. Pearlyclaws' heart was skipping like a horrible gym teacher at the end of term.

"You'll see, Uncle Shawn. You and your stupid friends – you'll see. By the time I have finished you'll all be scared of your own shadows and I will be the Emperor of Everywhere."

EMPEROR OF EVERYWHERE

A gentle breeze whistled over his loose nose – *ffeeep, ffeeep – ffeeep, ffeeep* – and started to give him a headache.

Then a light purple rain began to fall. 🐾

WICKED WOOL →

SECTION SEVEN

In which – oh, goodness me! – something else very worrying and terrible happens! I'm sure this will all end happily, but at the moment a beautiful albatross is in awful danger. Emergencia!

Out in the Pacific Ocean, a young albatross called Sophie was feeling tired. She had been flying through purple clouds, which had made her eyes water and caught in her feathers so that her wings felt exhausted. "I'll have to land for a while," she thought.

Landing is difficult for albatrosses, because they are so wonderfully big and have such magnificently wide wings that are difficult to fold out of the way. Sophie swept down lower and lower on her aching wings until she caught sight of what looked like a comfortable little island. "Ah... I will just rest there to clear my head and get my strength back and then I'll be on my way. *Flaps down, prepare for landing. Brace, brace, brace.*"

As gently as she could – she hadn't practised landing very much yet – she brought herself closer and closer to the surface of the water. She noticed the island looked rather odd. It had a strange purple glow and an older albatross might have avoided it, but Sophie decided, "Even a funny-looking island can't do me any harm."

Then she made her final landing announce-ment, just as her mother and father and big brother had taught her. "*Lower and lock landing gear, adjusting beak. Check, check, check.*" She glided down. The island glowed more brightly and nastily, but it was too late to turn back now.

Her big webbed feet touched the island and her gigantic wings began to fold. "Stowing flight gear. Oh, dear – that's not right..." Her beautiful, wide albatross feet were sinking into the island.

Oh, no!

She tried poking at the island with her long and amazing albatross beak and – oh, no! – the island wasn't an island at all. It was made of glowing purple wool, tangled together in a nasty lump.

In fact, this was some of the wool Pearlyclaws had stolen. He had spent months sprinkling it with purplonium and then throwing tangles of it into the sea and the Thames and other rivers!

What a truly awful man he is!

The more poor Sophie tried to pull her feet out of the wool, the more horribly trapped they became. Purplonium, the most evil element in the world, had made the wool wicked and alive enough to trap anything that touched it! *OH, NO!*

Sophie tried to flap her wings and lift herself

PURPLE WOOL

SOPHIE

free. *"Emergency take off! Emergency take off!"*
She was very brave and had been top of her class
in flying.

But it was no good. Albatrosses are so very
big and have such very long wings that they need
to run and run before they can lift themselves up
and into flight.

And Sophie couldn't run at all!

She was really trapped!

Lots of terrible ideas ran through her head
like upset horses. What would she do when she
got hungry? What would she do when she got
thirsty? What would she do if a shark came along
and wanted to eat her?

EMERGENCIA!

WIGGLING EARS

SECTION EIGHT

In which there is Uncle Shawn! He always knows what to do when children and grown-ups and animals are in trouble.

Brian Llama was standing outside at the back of the farmhouse wiggling his ears goodbye to the lady eagle as she circled high into the sky, going home. One of her long-clawed feet held a big ball of tummy fur that Brian hadn't really needed.

"Skeekeeweeee," she cried, dipping the big feathers at the end of one wing and then the other.

"That means *Thank you for giving some of your excellent fur to line my nest and may your beak always be sharp.*" Uncle Shawn tickled the top of Brian's head. "That is a very nice compliment, if you are an eagle and your beak is your knife and fork and spoon."

"Señora Eagle was very beautiful." Brian thought he would miss the eagle, even if she was a little bit terrifying and deadly.

Uncle Shawn winked. "Now we need to help the others clean up and have another look at the map the birds made for us of the Particularly Purple Problem."

Inside, Bill and the other llamas were cleaning away claw prints and web prints, loose feathers, crumbs and spatters of bird poo. The kitchen table was covered in a map that some of the birds had drawn by dipping their feet and beaks in strawberry jam, or mayonnaise, or custard – depending on what they liked best.

The birds had shown how many purple clouds they had seen over which countries and how much thicker the powdery purple was wherever there were people.

Unfortunately, Carlos and Guinevere Llama had licked quite a lot of the drawings and maps off the table because that seemed a delicious way to clean it.

"*Schlllllurrrp...* Oh, hello Uncle Shawn – doesn't the table look shiny?" Carlos grinned, finishing off a drawing of Edinburgh made in custard.

"*Sssssllllloopp.* Yes. This kind of cleaning is the best." Guinevere nodded as she licked off the list of towns that weren't yet completely covered in purple.

"Hmmm..." said Uncle Shawn while his hair wibbled as if it was trying to remember everything the llamas had just eaten. "Well, it would have helped to see everything again, but perhaps I can remember it."

"Oh, you foolish llamas." Ginalolobrigida trotted past wearing spare feathers in her fur from all the most beautiful birds. She was encouraging everyone else to clean faster by being extremely beautiful at them. "If only I could have feathers and soar above the countryside. I would show everyone how lovely a llama can be and bring joy to the world... Even more joy than Alfonso Aparador..." She sighed happily.

GINALOLOBRIGIDA

SOARING ABOVE THE COUNTRYSIDE

SHOWING EVERYONE HOW LOVELY A LLAMA CAN BE

BRINGING JOY TO THE WORLD

"I'm sorry Uncle Shawn." Bill had finally finished the washing up while Sam and Sky dried the plates and only played catch with a few of them, because otherwise Bill got nervous. Brushing the soap suds off his tummy fur with a fairly clean tea towel, Bill continued, "I wonder why none of the seagulls asked me what kind of pirate I am, or if I'm called Captain Silk Knees, or Black and White Bill the Terror of the Fifteen Seas."

CAPTAIN SILK KNEES

BLACK AND WHITE BILL, THE TERROR OF THE FIFTEEN SEAS

Nobody answered because – as we know – Bill's hat was lovely, but mostly made him look like a short, plump badger under a big hat, or maybe a mushroom with a long stripy nose.

Bill tilted his hat forward over his eyes, which always made him feel more like a sea dog. Or a sea badger. "Well?" Bill frowned. "This hat does make me look like a pirate, doesn't it?"

Uncle Shawn held Bill's paw in his hand while everyone else said things like:

"Oh, goodness me, yes – very piratey."

"You look more like a pirate than anyone else I have met today."

Or:

"Please, Señor Bill, you are extremely most like a pirate, yes indeed."

And – of course – as soon as they said these things which were kind but not true...

FF**BOO**MFF! FF**BOO**MFF!

Guinevere's, Carlos's and Brian's llama bottoms

all produced big billowing clouds of purple smoke. No matter how fast Brian ran away from his bottom, the cloud followed. After all, no matter how fast anyone runs, their bottom always stays right behind them.

TECHNICAL PROOF THAT IT IS IMPOSSIBLE TO RUN AWAY FROM YOUR OWN BOTTOM

Fig 1.

x

y

$x \infty$

$\frac{b}{?\$}$

$\emptyset$

And...

FFBOOMFF!

A delicate and shapely cloud of purple smoke appeared in a perfect and stylish *poooof* around Ginalolobrigida's bottom. And...

FFBOOMFF! FFBOOMFF!

Sam and Sky had to hold tea towels over their bottoms and run upstairs to change!

"I wish I had fur and didn't have to worry about my underpants exploding," yelled Sky as she ran.

While purple chaos broke out again, the freshly tidied kitchen was slowly covered in frightened hoof prints and spilled sugar and broken plates.

Uncle Shawn kept hold of Bill's paw and led him outside. "Well, Bill. I was not sure before, but now I know. There really is something wrong with the Living Fish Tree."

"But what is the Living Fish Tree? And how do you know it's ill? And what's wrong with my hat?"

The last question was the most important for Bill, so Uncle Shawn answered it first. "Your hat is wonderful and it makes you *feel* like a pirate. I am sure that you feel more like a pirate than many actual pirates."

"Even though I am a short, slightly rounded, young badger who has never been to sea?"

"No seafaring pirate with a ship and a pirate name and a special pirate song that his whole crew has to sing each morning would need to feel as much like a pirate as you do." Uncle Shawn tickled Bill's ears.

"But don't I look like a pirate?"

"Well, Bill, not really. But any sensible creature who paid attention could tell you are a badger who is full of adventures and bravery, who could

be a sea captain at any moment."

"So when everyone said I looked like a pirate they were lying?" Bill's ears wiggled with disappointment and he took off his hat.

"They were being nice, but they were not exactly telling the truth."

Bill's tail drooped. "What does that have to do with trees and fish, though?"

Uncle Shawn walked with Bill to their rocking chairs – a big one for Uncle Shawn and a badger-sized one for Bill. Uncle Shawn knew that rocking in his chair would make Bill feel happier.

"A very long time ago whenever anyone told a lie – even to stop someone's feelings being hurt – there would be a big bottom explosion of purple," Uncle Shawn began. "In the days long ago before underpants there would still be a whoosh and a big cloud of purple. This meant everyone knew when someone was lying. But it also meant no one could tell a fib to stop someone being upset."

Bill started to smile a little bit. "The way I tell Brian that he would be able to bite a swamp monster's knees and make it run away, so that he won't be so scared?"

"I am sure that Brian might be able to bite little monsters with little knees – but, yes, there might be other monsters who would bite Brian's knees first. If monsters existed at all. And we all tell Carlos the pancakes he makes are delicious – even if parts of them are on fire and parts of them are raw and parts of them are hairy from where he has pushed them about in the pan with his nose."

CARLOS'S FAVOURITE DISHES

1. CHARRED PANCAKES
WITH NOSE PRINTS AND CHERRIES

2. BANANA, TOFFEE AND CREAM PANCAKES
(THAT ARE ON FIRE)

3. CHARCOAL AND FLAME PANCAKES
WITH ADDED WATER AND TEA TOWEL

4. COLD PANCAKE BATTER
SERVED ON A BED OF ASH AND SEASONAL BERRIES

"He tries very hard to be a good cook."

"Anyway, long ago, people had become tired of having to stick their bottoms out of windows before they could even tell a nice fib. So everyone went to the Emperor of Everywhere and told him they would turn his throne into shelves and make him Emperor of Nowhere if he didn't help them. The Emperor was fed up of having burst trousers himself, so he ordered all the magicians of the world to find a solution." Uncle Shawn chuckled. "Well, none of the magicians had any luck and the people were just about to saw up the Emperor's throne when the oldest, oddest, hairiest magician, Herbert the Magnificent, shuffled into the palace and said, 'Done it.'"

"What had he done?" asked Bill, his whiskers tingling.

"He had shouted horrible lies and insults at an innocent scone for years and years until it suddenly went purple and started to glow. It had turned into what he called purplonium, the worst substance in the world! That wasn't what he wanted at all, so he hid the purplonium in a secret cave where it wouldn't harm anybody and tried again.

INSULTS + SCONE = PURPLONIUM

"He had also spent years yelling good lies and compliments at a bucket of sea water until a strange, eight-armed, tiny tree started to grow in it, all rainbow-coloured and shiny. When he was near the tree and told a lie, his underpants didn't explode. He said he had released what he called a baby tree into the ocean and was hoping it would grow big enough to save everybody's underpants.

COMPLIMENTS + BUCKET OF SEA WATER = TINY TREE

"Nobody believed him, of course. But, slowly, fewer and fewer pants exploded until one day, anyone could say anything they liked. And sailors began to tell tales of a wonderful rainbow-shining tree, deep in the ocean, which seemed to have fish for leaves – the Living Fish Tree.

"After a while everyone forgot about the exploding underpants problem, because it was too embarrassing to put in history books. So they forgot about the Living Fish Tree and the purplonium, too."

Bill rocked gently in his chair and, although he was still not wearing his hat, he looked much happier. "How do you know about this if everyone has forgotten?"

Uncle Shawn's hair wibbled happily. "When I was a little, tiny baby boy I always wanted to go on adventures, but I was too small, so as soon as I could talk I started asking the animals and birds and insects and fish about their adventures. After they learned to trust me, they told me about all the places in the world and all the amazing things they saw and all the oldest stories."

"So if pants are exploding again, something must be wrong with the Living Fish Tree!"

"Exactly!" Uncle Shawn laughed. "The only worse thing than the Living Fish Tree getting sick would be if someone had found the purplonium and started using its wicked powers!"

Bill said, "That's just the kind of thing Pearlyclaws would try. Thank goodness he's safely locked up by now."

"I do hope so." Uncle Shawn clapped his hands. "And I think we have to go on an adventure now to save the Living Fish Tree – and everybody's pants." He winked at Bill. "Very soon you will be an exploring badger who has been underneath the sea, which is much harder than just floating about on top of it."

Bill thought swimming and floating on top

of the water was much better than diving under it and getting it up your big stripy nose. (If you happened to have a big, stripy nose.) Boats were meant to stay on top of the water, too – and submarines had always seemed a bit too exciting for Bill. He didn't like the thought of sinking down under the waves in a big heavy metal craft and being close to mysterious ocean creatures... "You don't have a submarine do you, Uncle Shawn?"

"Dearie me, no. Where would I keep a submarine? It would mean we had no room in the cupboards for extra biscuits. No, we will go under the water just by ourselves."

NO ROOM FOR BISCUITS

"By ourselves?" asked Bill in a voice that had gone quite squeaky with surprise.

"Yes, yes... We will walk out underneath the water for a few hours, or days – as long as the adventure takes. We may have to search many seas and oceans before we find where the Living Fish Tree is."

Bill couldn't hold his breath for a minute, never mind a day! "But Uncle Shawn, how?!"

Uncle Shawn smiled. "I'll show you. And you will have a magnificent adventure no pirate could even imagine!" He squeezed Bill's paw. "Come on Bill. Let's start! How do you start a pudding race?" asked Uncle Shawn, standing up and heading back to the farmhouse.

"You sago!" answered Bill as he scampered after his best friend. But even though telling jokes always made him happy, he still couldn't help thinking, "Oh dearie, dearie, dearie me...! Under the sea...! Me...!" 🐾

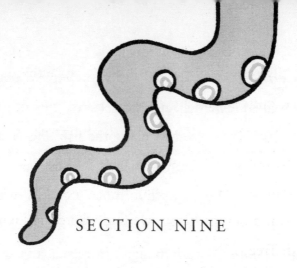

SECTION NINE

In which there is an especially wonderful

octopus. But she might need Uncle Shawn!

Oh, yes indeed! She might need Uncle Shawn

to come and help her a lot! And soon!

Deep down underneath the Pacific Ocean, not far from where Sophie the albatross was being very worried, a giant and marvellous octopus was feeling very poorly. Her massive rounded head and body rested on the ocean floor, where everything was dark, dark, dark. Usually, her eight long powerful arms stretched up high to the places where the water was light and blue-green and beautiful, but now they just drifted sadly, or flopped onto the seabed. The delicate and sensitive tips of the octopus's limbs used to tickle the fish and wave to all her many, many shoals of friends, but not any more. The gigantunormous octopus usually glowed with a bright rainbow kind of light that shimmered and changed from red, to blue, to bandaroon, to green, to himmelac, to milky-oople-urple and so on. But now her wonderful light was failing.

Happy young fish used to play and grow in her enormous arms. Strange sea creatures would sleep in her care. For hundreds and hundreds of years sea beings had been born under the protection of the octopus. She was the greatest wonder of the under-sea world. She was, of course, the Living Fish Tree!

But now the huge creature no longer flipped and swished her limbs about and made rainbows of colour spread for miles under the ocean. Her kind eyes didn't wink at the passing seahorses, or

watch fish eggs
hatch and jellyfish drift and turtles
row along with their big paddle arms.

While the skies above filled with drifting clouds of purple and millions of pants exploded on dry land, the streams of purple in the ocean seemed to be really hurting the Living Fish Tree. The seaweed around the marvellous beast was withering. Many creatures worried that soon they would have nowhere to hide when the bigger sea beasts swam along to eat them.

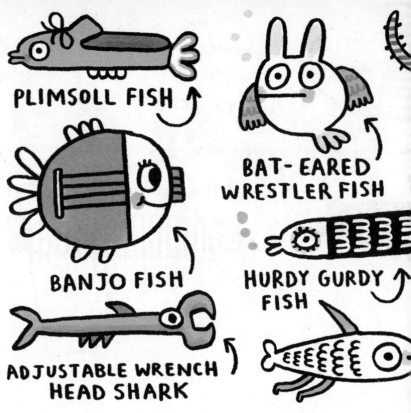

PLIMSOLL FISH

BAT-EARED
WRESTLER FISH

BANJO FISH

HURDY GURDY
FISH

ADJUSTABLE WRENCH
HEAD SHARK

The tiny fish worried that they would have to move away and do the rest of their growing up out in the big scary ocean. Plimsoll fish, bat-eared wrestler fish, horse-faced pontoon fish, hurdy gurdy fish – all the kinds of fish – began swimming nervously away to find shelter some-where else.

Meanwhile, slowly, in the distance all around

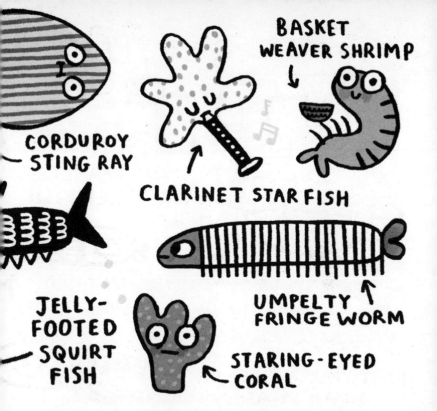

CORDUROY STING RAY

BASKET WEAVER SHRIMP

CLARINET STAR FISH

JELLY-FOOTED SQUIRT FISH

UMPELTY FRINGE WORM

STARING-EYED CORAL

the Living Fish Tree the frightened sea beings could just make out big dark shapes with pointy fins. Every now and then there was a flash of teeth. The clarinet starfish and the umpelty fringe worms, the jelly-footed squirtfish – everyone couldn't help thinking: sharks!

Oh, no!

Emergencia! 🐾

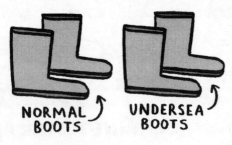

NORMAL BOOTS

UNDERSEA BOOTS

SECTION TEN

In which there are lots of boots – and an especially brave llama. There are also some buckets.

The next day, Sam and Sky were practising holding their breath down on the beach at Shoogeldy Bay.

"I wonder how far we're going to have to go," said Sky, letting out a breath and looking out at all the wide blue miles of sea that stretched out to meet the sky.

"I don't know," said Sam, holding Sky's hand. He was feeling a bit scared about a great big sea journey. "I'm sure Uncle Shawn has a plan, though."

"Or at least a bit of a plan…"

"Or the beginning of the start of a plan..."

"I wonder what a Living Fish Tree is," said Sky.

"Uncle Shawn said we would recognise it when we saw it, but I'm not sure that's true," said Sam.

"Uncle Shawn doesn't ever tell lies though, does he?" said Sky, suddenly realising this was something else unusual about Uncle Shawn.

"No, I don't think he ever does... Not even little ones..."

And the thought of Uncle Shawn being so nice and unusual and brave and funny and rushing to help people and animals with not exactly the whole of a plan, but a bit of one, made them feel an adventure might be fun. So they ran up and down and then held their breath some more.

Meanwhile, Brian Llama was trying to be braver than he ever had been.

"Now, Brian," said Uncle Shawn, patting Brian's long llama neck and tickling his lovely llama fur. "You are the bravest llama in the world. You are so scared of everything that you have to be braver than anyone, just to get out of bed."

Brian blushed. "Well… Perhaps and maybe."

Uncle Shawn smiled. "I think you should be in charge of the farm while I am away saving everyone's underpants with Bill and Sam and Sky. I am sure that the other llamas will help you."

He smiled at the other llamas, while they all stared at Brian as if they would be much better at everything than their worried llama friend.

"Carlos," said Uncle Shawn, "you can make breakfast pancakes for everyone while we're away."

"Yes, I shall do this." Carlos nodded proudly.

"And maybe some of them will not be on fire," said Guinevere, and she giggled.

"If they do catch fire you can put out the flames with jam. I always do," suggested Uncle Shawn, and then he grinned.

"I will be even more beautiful when you return. It will be something for you to look forward to," announced Ginalolobrigida Llama. "And I will wear my strongest mascara and use my wonderfully long eyelashes to blink away any purpleness that comes near us." She tilted her head to a glamorous angle and fluttered her eyelashes so that everyone could feel the small breeze they very definitely did make.

Then Uncle Shawn clapped his hands together and reminded them all, "Bill has baked lots and lots for you to eat. Don't shout at the scones.

THINGS NOT TO DO TO SCONES

1. SHOUT AT THEM

2. WASH THEM IN HOT, SOAPY WATER

3. THROW THEM AT A WASP

4. USE THEM AS A BOOKMARK

There is a whole sack of apples in the pantry and a sack of carrots, too. And I have put some nice, sweet hay in your barns."

"How long, please and thank you, do you think you will be away, Señor Uncle Shawn?" asked Brian, his voice trembling a bit. He didn't want to be in charge for more than ten minutes, maybe only eight.

"We will be as quick as we can. And I am sure the llama farm is in safe hooves with you."

"I do not exactly know this…" mumbled Brian and patted the grass with his hoof. "I will try."

"Wonderful!" laughed Uncle Shawn, and his hair wibbled happily. "I knew you would be brave!"

"Si! I know I am most brave!" said Brian in his loudest voice. But then—

FFBOOMFF!

Oh, dear! Another purple powdery cloud and a bit less bottom fur for Brian.

Brian sighed. "If things go on like this, I shall have a bald bottom and that will be most very extremely sad and cold in the winter…"

Ginalolobrigida fluttered her eyelashes powerfully and Uncle Shawn waggled his long arms and his long hair and the purple cleared a little bit.

"Goodness! It is high time we started our adventure! Don't worry Brian, when we have sorted everything out we can knit you some llama trousers until your fur grows back!"

LLAMAS!

DO YOU HAVE A →
POSTERIOR PROBLEM?

TOO MUCH AIR AND NOT ENOUGH HAIR ON YOUR PRECIOUS LLAMA BOTTOM?

PROBLEM SOLVED!

← WITH LUXURY LLAMA POSTERIOR PANTALOONS!

AMAZING FOR GRAZING AND STARGAZING!

order 12 pairs and get half a pair FREE!

And off Uncle Shawn went, to put on his Undersea Clothes, which were...

Just like his usual clothes, only with much heavier boots carved out of stone. They were almost too heavy to walk in and would keep him from bobbing to the surface when he was under the water.

Uncle Shawn had ordered another pair of Undersea Boots from the Big Badger Supply Company and had given them to Bill that morning. The huge, heavy package made the postman need a cup of tea.

Uncle Shawn also went to his Everything Cupboard and found the Undersea Boots he had worn when he was six and the Undersea Boots he had worn when he was seven. He thought they should fit Sky and Sam very nicely. During the night he had also gone out into the garden and cut big square face windows in two buckets to make two undersea helmets for Sam and Sky. Then he had made a badger-sized helmet out of two more buckets fastened together to make enough room for a beautiful long stripy nose.

Uncle Shawn went outside and danced for a while, flapping his long arms like long wings and throwing back his head and hopping delicately. This was part of his plan, although if you had seen him you might just have thought he was only having fun. In fact this was a special dance to summon help from the seas and oceans. He hopped and waved and wobbled out the message: "UNCLE SHAWN NEEDS GARGANTUNORMOUS HELP. COME QUICKLY!"

Of course, Uncle Shawn was having fun, too – he loved dancing. And he was looking forward to seeing which sea creature came to help him. He knew it would be a big one.

Then Uncle Shawn set off for the beach. With the stone Undersea Boots on his feet and two more pairs in his backpack, and the buckets and the other backpacks in his arms, he could only move very slowly and sounded like several knights in armour falling down stone steps. By the time he reached Shoogeldy Bay he was hot and out of breath, but he felt much better when he saw Sam and Sky and Badger Bill already standing at the water's edge.

"Hello, everyone!" Uncle Shawn called and waved his arms. Then he dropped everything onto the sand with a tremendous din. He smiled. "That's lucky. Everything has landed on the

ground, which is where I was going to put it."

Bill scratched his nose. "The ground is always where things land."

"Really? My things land all over the place." Uncle Shawn chuckled. "I have backpacks with sandwiches in them and apples and biscuits and lots and lots of packets of powdered air. No one can go under the sea without powdered air, or lots and lots of equipment that we don't have. And, of

patented
POWDERED
UNDERSEA
AIR

THE *finest* AIR FROM SWISS MOUNTAINS

EXPLORE LONGER with powdered air that's STRONGER

IDEAL FOR ALL
• FISH FRIENDS
• WHALE MATES
• EXPLORERS OF THE DEEP

(ALSO AVAILABLE IN PINE FOREST)

course, sea creatures need powdered water before they can go on land..." He winked. "These buckets are to go over your heads." He tickled one of Bill's ears. "And then we can start walking under the sea to find the Living Fish Tree and make her well."

"Are you sure that won't be dangerous?" asked Bill.

"Everything will be fine. I promise." Then Uncle Shawn handed out the backpacks – one, two, three – and gave the twins their Undersea Boots. "Now we will all swallow lots of powdered air. When you breathe out underwater it will fill your bucket helmets and keep out the water so it won't go into your ears. It always feels very tickly to have ears full of water." He gave Bill the special badger-shaped helmet and made sure it was comfy. "I like having tickly ears – so I don't need a helmet." Uncle Shawn grinned.

And so Sam and Sky put on their stone boots and then their bucket helmets and looked out through their face windows.

"This is going to be fun," said Sam.

"I know," said Sky. Both the twins felt a bit nervous, though, and so they held hands.

Bill looked up at the happy face of his best friend Uncle Shawn and saw the way his hair was wibbling – as if it couldn't wait to be under the sea. "Well, if Uncle Shawn isn't scared, I suppose I don't need to be either," he thought to himself.

Then he munched down a big pawful of powdered air – which tasted like fresh strawberries.

Sam and Sky also swallowed handfuls of air. Then Uncle Shawn and his three friends put on their backpacks and marched very slowly and carefully and heavily out into the sea.

The water was a bit cold as it crept up their legs and over their bottoms and tummies and chests and then – oooooh – Bill was right underwater because he was the smallest.

"This feels very odd," Bill thought. "I'm not sure if I like it." The view out of his helmet window was very blue and strange and he could see the fur on his arms waving like seaweed. "Oh, dear."

Bill started to hold his breath. He didn't quite believe that the powdered air was going to work. But because Uncle Shawn was his best friend and said everything would be all right, Bill kept on walking, further and further away from the beach... 🐾

VERY WICKED WOOL →

SECTION ELEVEN

In which there is an incredibly brave albatross
– you can guess who that is. And there is an
incredibly evil human – you can guess who that
is. And there is some sliding – and some poo.

While Badger Bill was under the North Sea, finding out how to breathe powdered air, Sophie the wonderful albatross was still stuck. She was far away, floating on the Pacific Ocean with her feet trapped in the wicked wool that Pearlyclaws had infected with purplonium and then thrown into the water to make trouble for sea creatures.

"*Landing gear malfunction, landing gear*

malfunction." She sighed to herself. "Oh, dear. Mum and Dad never warned me about Purple Problems."

Albatrosses can fly as easily as you sit in a chair and can glide along for years at a time without ever landing. She missed being up in the air. And she missed her mum and dad who were off flying and gliding magnificently hundreds of miles away and didn't know she needed them.

Sophie shook her head sadly. "It's getting dark." She could feel that one of her feet was stuck right through the tangled wool and was waggling in the water beneath. And also in the water beneath she thought she could see dark shapes. They looked hungry!

HUNGRY SHAPE

"No. I won't panic," she thought. Pilots have to be very calm in emergencies and albatrosses are some of the finest bird pilots. "There's nothing I can do now… I should get some rest so that I will feel stronger and know what to do when the sun comes up." A single tear ran down her big beak. "Oh, but I'm too worried to sleep. I do hope someone comes to rescue me."

Before Sophie let her head drop and closed her eyes, she noticed a faint light shimmering with lovely rainbow colours very far below. When she looked at it, she felt as if things might get a bit better soon. Her feathers seemed cosier, too. In fact, she stopped being quite so scared and went to sleep. She didn't know about the Living Fish Tree, but if she had, she might have guessed that she was floating right above it. The giant, kind, magical octopus was very weak, but she was still trying to help Sophie as much as she could with the little bit of strength she had left.

• • •

Meanwhile, Pearlyclaws was sitting in his horrible smelly chair in his horrible smelly Sitting Room of Evil. His monitors showed him dreams from humans and creatures all over the world. Sophie was dreaming about clouds and soaring free, but Pearlyclaws wasn't watching that. Instead, he was sniggering to himself and fiddling with a little metal box.

He was happily imagining how many sea

creatures were getting tangled in purplonium wool. He was overjoyed that purplonium was creeping into the water everywhere too and hurting the Living Fish Tree. And the more purplonium he released, the more purplonium there seemed to be. Every little bit of it told every other little bit about all the wicked things it was doing and the wickedness made it grow. Pearlyclaws was delighted that he had more and more purplonium in his big jar. Every time he threw purplonium into a lake or a river for wicked reasons, the purplonium he had left doubled and tripled in size. Every time he had an especially nasty thought, it would shine and slide about as if it was delighted too.

But even this much wickedness wasn't enough for Pearlyclaws! He was moving on to the next part of his Particularly Purple Plot! That little metal box he was playing with wasn't just a box! It was a remote control!

Now what could it be controlling?!

Helpful lights to guide llama children home wherever it is dark?

Or automatic pie machines that give pies to hungry people?

Or remote control submarines that swim out across the Pacific to make sure albatrosses are safe?

No...

Nothing as nice as that.

Pearlyclaws hissed horribly, "Now I will get you, Uncle Shawn! My purplonium will get you! I will have my revenge! Your stupid happiness is over!"

The purplonium hissed back at him in its jar.

Pearlyclaws smiled with his grey prison teeth. Then he giggled, which sounded like a donkey being tickled – *eeh-hoo-hee-hoo-eeh-hoo-eeh-haw*. His loose nose whistled in reply – *ffeeep, ffeeep – ffeeep, ffeeep.*

It was all so dreadful that Katie and Bernard Pinktail, who had been trying to clean Pearlyclaws' shoes, felt sick and had to run away.

WARM HILL OF POO

They spent the rest of their evening sliding up and down a warm hill of poo to cheer themselves up. That's how horrible Pearlyclaws was – he made rats who like poo-sliding feel sick! 🐾

SECTION TWELVE

In which there are – oh dear me! – so many
teeth. And they're getting closer! Definitely
don't read this bit in the bath.

In Shoogeldy Bay, everyone was trying to get used to being underwater and breathing Uncle Shawn's powdered air. (Never go underwater without it.) Their first few breaths had filled their bucket helmets and kept the water out, just the way Uncle Shawn had promised, so they didn't have tickly ears. And now every time they breathed out, long streams of bubbles sparkled up to the surface.

It was hard to lift their big stone boots, but

Sam and Sky thought it was fun, too. As they made their way deeper under the waves, a seahorse swam right up and stuck its tongue out at Sky. Then it swam and winked at Sam. Sam shouted "Hooo! Seahorse!" in big bubbles that everyone could hear. The bubbles made the seahorse dart away and bow to Uncle Shawn. Uncle Shawn bowed back and wriggled his fingers happily. It seemed he really did know all the animals on Earth – even the watery ones.

The seahorse didn't say hello to Bill, because our badger pal wasn't enjoying himself at all. Holding his breath was making Bill feel dizzy and his fur was puffing out and wiggling in strange ways, just the way your hair does in the swimming baths, only all over. Bill didn't look as elegant as he wanted to. He hadn't got the hang of his stone boots, either. He had always wanted to be a famous, brave explorer, but he didn't feel like one and he felt ashamed of himself. By the time it was sunset in the dry world, Bill was tired and miserable. Inside his helmet, his ears were drooping and his tail would have drooped too if it hadn't been so puffed out by the water.

Uncle Shawn saw that Bill was unhappy and held his paw. "Ah, Bill. Don't worry. You'll soon love the water like a real pirate." A flock of flounders flipped out of the mud and giggled at them. "And look. Everything is about to get much better and more exciting!" Uncle Shawn pointed his long finger towards a dark dot that was almost too small to notice, even smaller than this full stop.

But the dot was getting bigger – fast.

"Is that a fish?" asked Bill.

"A very special fish, yes. I danced a Summoning Dance last night and I hoped that he would feel my message with his clever nose. His nose is even

more full of cleverness than your own."

The dot was getting bigger. In fact, it wasn't a dot any more, it was more like a big, dark oval shape. And everyone could see that part of it was moving from side to side, as if it had a tail that was moving back and forth powerfully...

"What's that?" asked Sky in speech bubbles.

"It's coming straight towards us." Sam was pointing towards the growing shape. "It's almost as if it knows we're here."

"Oh, he knows." Uncle Shawn nodded. "In my dance I said we would come this way."

Bill looked up at Uncle Shawn through his face window. "It's not the whale that swallowed Pearlyclaws, is it?"

"No, no. A whale is not a fish, it is a mammal. You wouldn't want to call Mr Hub a fish, he would be most offended. No, that is a fish coming towards us, a fish which is not quite as large as a whale. Not quite..."

The shape was even bigger now and definitely had a very strong, lashing tail – and a tall fin on its back... Oh, dear...

Sky said in a huge bubble of sound, "That looks just like a—"

Sam said in another huge bubble of sound, "Oh my goodness, isn't that a—"

And Bill suddenly found that he could breathe powdered air really, really well, because he breathed in a gigantunormous breath and yelled, "SHAAAAAAAARK!"

By now the gigantic shape was ever so close and, yes, it was a huge shark! It had pointy fins and sandpapery grey sides and little dark eyes and – oh no! – gigantunormous teeth.

Everyone was able to see its teeth because, as it drifted to a halt and stared at them all, it opened its mouth!

The shark's jaws were so huge that Bill could have walked in between them without having to duck. (Although he really might not have wanted to.) Bill's fur and whiskers shivered with fright. "Aaaahhh! You told a shark we'd be here!?!"

Even if Uncle Shawn had stepped in past those massive jaws and past those white, white teeth that were bigger than the biggest slice of cake you can imagine, he wouldn't have had to duck his head the tiniest bit. That's how big the shark was.

But the shark was just gently wiggling its snout and drifting peacefully, always looking back at them. It was letting the current play over its gills so that it could breathe. (Sharks can't keep still because they need water to flow over their gills so they can breathe. This makes them restless and means they get in trouble a lot when they're at school.)

But no one was thinking about how difficult life was for shark teachers. Sam and Sky and especially Bill were all staring up at the shark and shouting, *"EMERGENCIA!"*

As they did this, Uncle Shawn stepped much closer to the shark.

"EVEN MORE EMERGENCIA!"

Then he bowed politely and the shark opened its mouth even wider.

"WAAAAAAAAA!"

Then Uncle Shawn reached out and gently tickled the gigantunormous shark's gigantunormous nose.

"NOOOOOOOO! WAAAAAAAAAAAA! EMERGENCIAAAAAAAA!" shouted everyone.

But the shark didn't eat Uncle Shawn, not a bit. He just rolled over onto his back and floated beside Uncle Shawn so that Uncle Shawn could reach across and tickle some of his pale, massive belly.

Uncle Shawn winked an undersea wink. "It's a good thing sharks are used to screaming, or you might have frightened him. Come and help me rub his tummy – he likes that. After all, not many people ever do tickle sharks."

Very gingerly, the twins edged forward, but only by one step. Bill stood still, his fur so puffed up with fright that he looked like a black and white beach ball with scared eyes.

But then the shark flipped back over! And then it slipped past Uncle Shawn as quick as oiled eels and darted over to poor Bill! Bill just had time to let loose a huge bubble that said "EEEP!"

Then Bill disappeared – gobbled up right inside the shark's mouth!

Oh, no!

But before anyone could shout, "EMERGEN-CIA!" the shark opened his mouth again and left Bill standing just where he had been, only with his fur all smooth and neat and looking extra-elegant. Shark spit had smoothed his fur down and got rid of all the tickly bubbles caught in it. Bill looked much better. And he was no longer wearing his bucket helmet. The shark was chewing that up like chewing gum, just because he could.

"Oof!" said Bill, who hadn't ever expected to be in the warm, dark inside of a shark's mouth. "Whhaaagh!" Surprise had made all his words disappear.

But then he looked down at his shark's-tooth-combed fur and its coating of glossy shark spit that had made it look very beautiful. "Oh... Umm... Thank you. Umm... Mr Shark." No water was tickling in his ears, because they were covered in shark spit. He was astonished to find that he felt much more like a brave and dashing explorer.

The shark smiled in a way that was both nice and horrifying. Then he spoke with a deep, wet, sharp kind of voice, "You looked uncomfortable – and I know that my saliva is very good at making things smooth. And easy to swallow." He grinned alarmingly.

Bill tried not to think about the shark swallowing anything.

The shark chuckled. "What is your name, tiny snack? I mean, tiny land creature."

BADGER SNACK

SHARK SNACK

"B-B-B-Bill." Bill held out one trembling paw.

"I'm afraid I can't shake hands. I don't have any. At least not outside my tummy." The shark winked again with one of its glossy black eyes.

"Nnnggaa..." said Bill. Then he managed to wave hello. "And ... ah ... what's your name?"

"I'm called WAAAAAAA!!!" said the shark. "At least that's what most creatures call me when they see me. My real name is Timothy." And then, as the sunset up above the waves turned the watery light all red, Timothy smiled so broadly that his teeth shone like, well ... like the most gigantunormous teeth that you can imagine and then a bit bigger than that. 🐾

SECTION THIRTEEN

In which there are – oh dear me! – scary

nightmares! And there is purplonium! And

a lot more of Brian Llama than usual!

As the sun set behind the Pandrumdroochit Hills, Brian Llama was feeling quite proud of himself. He had made sure that the farmhouse was tidy after dinner and everyone had helped him to carry fresh water and lemonade to the drinking troughs. He had fluffed up the straw in the other llamas' barns so that it would be extra comfy and had even laid a single mint-flavoured scone on each pillow, in case anyone felt peckish overnight. Being so busy and thinking so much about other llamas meant that he didn't have any time to worry. He hadn't counted his hooves even once in the whole day.

By the time he was ready for bed he felt tired but happy. He flopped onto his own pile of straw, closed his eyes and snuggled his long llama nose against his pillow. Sleep rushed in, ready to carry him off to Dreamland. He just had time to mumble, "Buenas noches, Señor Claude. Sleep well." And then he was snoring as wonderfully as anyone can who has a long llama nose.

Over in Guinevere and Carlos's barn, Guinevere was holding her favourite toy hippopotamus and had finished her mug of hot milk, which Carlos had made for her because he was feeling kind. Then she cleaned every one of her big llama teeth and went to bed. Carlos was wearing his Capitán Fantástico pyjamas. He didn't need pyjamas at all because he was already covered in fur, but the Capitán was

CAPITÁN FANTÁSTICO

✦✦✦ VS ✦✦✦

TAPIRS FROM OUTER SPACE!

HIS BIGGEST ADVENTURE YET!

¡MAYOR AVENTURA AÚN!

LONG NOSES AGAINST LONGER NOSES!
IN SPACE! (sometimes)

FEATURING: LOS HERMANOS JAGUAR!
MORE SONGS! MORE FIGHTS!
MORE FAMILY RECIPES!

WHO IS FANTÁSTICO'S <u>REAL</u> FATHER?
✶✶ **AND WHY? FIND OUT IN...** ✶✶
CAPITÁN FANTÁSTICO VS TAPIRS FROM OUTER SPACE!

his favourite llama superhero. Both our llama friends looked happy as they trumpeted llama snores down their llama noses and headed off into their dreams.

Ginalolobrigida was always late going to bed

126

because it took her so long to remove her make-up and then apply her night creams and brush all of her fur with 1,000 strokes to make it shine. Finally, she snuggled into her hammock, closed her eyes and put on her Luscious Looks Sleep Mask. She fully expected to dream of exciting meals and film star parties with the llama superstar Alfonso Aparador. Soon she also began to snore, thundering away so loudly that the slates on the barn roof shivered.

But, as you will remember, Sylvester Pearlyclaws was waiting in his Supervillain Lair, watching the llamas' dreams. Our llama pals had already drunk tea and lemonade and just plain water that was full of teeny tiny traces of purplonium, so they were full of teeny tiny traces of purplonium too. This meant Pearlyclaws could see everything they saw when they fell asleep. Every bit of purplonium on Earth sent messages to every other bit and every bit of purplonium listened when he whispered to his big jar of purplonium.

Once upon a time, of course, Herbert the Magnificent had created purplonium by yelling at a scone until it became evil. He didn't know what to do with the scone – which was now glowing and purple and horribly wicked – so he hid it away in a deep cave where it stayed for many centuries.

Then one day Pearlyclaws was hiding from the police in an ancient library full of secret books. As he lay under a table, he noticed the world's only copy of Herbert the Magnificent's diary and read it until the policemen went away. The diary told Pearlyclaws about purplonium and where to find the cave where it was hidden! That's how the wickedest man on Earth found the wickedest thing on Earth. Oh, no!

And now, long after his only visit to a library, Pearlyclaws whispered terrible words to his purplonium and watched Ginalolobrigida dream she was saving Alfonso Aparador from bandits by doing high karate kicks.

LLAMA KARATE

EASY self-defence for llamas (and vicuñas, possibly ponies)

CROUCHING LLAMA, HIDDEN LLAMA

TWISTING DOUBLE HIP LUNGE

CROSSED HOOVES

SPITTING LLAMA, BITING LLAMA

FLYING CRANE LEAP

PLUS!

- USE OF EARS FOR BALANCE
- EXTRA TAIL POSITIONS
- MASCARA FOR BEGINNERS

Next Instalment — HOVERING, EAR STRIKES AND INVISIBILITY

Pearlyclaws watched Guinevere dream she was holding a tiny pink hippo in the palm of her hand and tickling its cute tummy while it smiled. Carlos was chasing footballs made of doughnuts across the skin of a giant purple jelly and whistling the Peruvian national anthem. A crowd of admiring llamas watched him.

But as Pearlyclaws whispered to the purplonium, it glowed brighter and brighter and everything began to change...

Ginalolobrigida tripped over her dream hooves and Alfonso Aparador stared at her and said, "Your eyeshadow makes you look like a swamp clown." Even though his voice sounded lovely, Ginalolobrigida felt very hurt. She wasn't having a dream at all – she was having a nightmare! *Una pesadilla!*

Soon Carlos's dream was making him feel more and more exhausted. Then the doughnut footballs started to chase him and Capitán Fantástico joined in. "I would never have eaten doughnuts if I knew they might eat me back," thought Carlos, as he ran away. Then lots of burning pancakes arrived and started to shout, "Why do you keep setting us on fire?" His dream was a nightmare! A bad *pesadilla*!

In her dream Guinevere was now being tickled by hundreds of tiny, wriggly pink hippos. This was so much fun that Guinevere loved it. But back in London, Pearlyclaws started to poke the purplonium with his fingers and slowly the hippos started to stare at her with scary pink eyes. Another *pesadilla*!

Then Pearlyclaws whispered to the purplonium, "That was fun, but let's make Brian scared now. He's so terrified and stupid – it's wonderful." Pearlyclaws knew Brian was the most nervous llama in Scotland – and anywhere else. A really bad nightmare might force him to cry for a week, or frighten his fur so much it would turn white, or all kinds of other things that would make Pearlyclaws giggle with the sound of someone grating an evil gym shoe.

Pearlyclaws could see that Brian was dreaming he had lots and lots of llama brothers and sisters. He was dancing the Marinera dance

with them and rubbing noses and cooking mountains of delicious *puka pikante* with spicy potatoes and peanuts. Brian didn't really have any brothers or sisters, but he'd always wanted some.

But then, as Pearlyclaws and the purplonium watched the Brian monitor, Brian started to have too many brothers and sisters. Dream llamas were arriving from east, south, north and west and all the directions in between. More and more llamas, until Brian's dream felt squashed and hot. He was having a *pesadilla*!

Emergencia!

In fact, his nightmare was so worrying that he woke up.

Of course, once he was awake he knew the nightmare would go away. He rolled over and wiggled his nose and opened his eyes and everything was absolutely—

Oh, no...

EMERGENCIA!!!

Everything was absolutely awful!

Hundreds of strange llamas were in Brian's barn! They were standing behind him, lying along the roof beams, sitting beside his bed, sticking their heads up through his bed straw! They were everywhere!

And they were all staring at him with nasty purple eyes!

As if this wasn't bad enough, every one of the llamas looked the same – and seemed really familiar.

Brian couldn't quite think where he might have seen that face before…

And then he realised – he saw that face every time he looked in a mirror! The llamas were all Brians!

And just as he thought this they all said, **"HELLO, BRIAN LLAMA! WE'RE BRIAN LLAMA!"** Then they blinked their scary purple eyes!

Oh, no!

It was a horrible, horrible nightmare.

But Brian was awake! 🐾

SECTION FOURTEEN

In which there is a scary laugh and a scary journey
but also lots and lots of help and kindness.

Meanwhile Badger Bill was having a big enough adventure to make sure his picture would be included in the list of Famous Badger Explorers. If he survived!

Timothy the Extremely Great White Shark asked him, "Would you like to climb inside my mouth?" Then he grinned while Bill tried not to scream.

"Now, Timothy," interrupted Uncle Shawn. "Don't tease poor Bill. He has never met an Extremely Great White Shark before. Or any other kind of shark. He thinks you want him for your supper."

Timothy laughed a huge laugh that sounded like somebody sharpening knives with a lawnmower. "Of course I will not eat you, tiny landbeast. I will never eat a friend of Uncle Shawn."

This made Sam and Sky smile. They were starting to like the monstrous shark – but they still held each other's hands, just in case.

Bill was trying to believe that the twinkle in the huge shark's eye was cheerful.

Uncle Shawn tapped the enormous shark on its nose with one of his long fingers. "No more teasing. Maybe later if you are nice and kind to him, Bill will take off his sea boots and run up and down your tummy with his warm, tickly paws."

"Mmmm…" Timothy wagged his huge tail. This made everyone sway back and forth in the water like kites in the wind, with only their Undersea Boots holding them down. "I would like that very much. But right now I am glad that you did the Summoning Dance. I have come to tell you that tangling nasty stuff is floating all over the oceans and seas, and animals and fish are being hurt. And the sky is turning purple and we don't know why, but we do know it's making the sea too dark for us. And the rain sounds peculiar and the water feels odd against my nose."

"But what about the Living Fish Tree?" asked Sky. She wanted to understand more about that mysterious creature.

Timothy turned to her as fast as fast, with a flash of teeth and a glimmer from his black eyes. Sky couldn't help saying, "WAAAAAAA!!!"

This made the monstrous shark giggle with a noise that gave everyone goosebumps. "You can call me WAAAAAAA!!! if you like. But Timothy is a bit quieter." He winked. "How do you know about the Living Fish Tree, little screaming landbeast?"

BRAVE TWINS

"She's called Sky!" shouted Sam as bravely as he could manage, because he always protected his sister, just as she always protected him.

"Mmmm... Sky..." Timothy wagged his tail a little. "What you call the Living Fish Tree is a giant, wise, wonderful, magical octopus and she helps the whole ocean. She's like our heart and she's very, very ill, maybe dying." The shark looked as sad as his massive teeth would let him and turned to Uncle Shawn. "We need you to help her the way you have helped so many of us."

"Uncle Shawn helps sea creatures, too?" asked Bill.

"Oh yes. He saved my life. I was only a very small shark – maybe eight or nine feet long – and I was tangled in some fishing net. He swam out and got me free."

"He saved my life, too, when I was kid-napped," said Bill and then he reached out his hand and tickled the shark's nose gently. It felt a bit like tickling the front of a submarine.

"But Uncle Shawn" – the shark sounded really worried – "the Living Fish Tree is in the Pacific Ocean. That's very far from Scotland and we don't have much time. So we need to hurry."

"How will we get there? That's thousands of miles away!" yelled the twins in big excited bubbles.

"Well," said Timothy. "If you tried to ride on top of us you might be swept away, we'll be swimming very fast for a very long time…"

"Us?" asked Sky.

"Me and Mum." The shark smiled.

"Your mum?!" Everyone tried to imagine how big Timothy's mum would be, just as a huge shadow swept gracefully closer and closer, like an ocean liner…

"Goodness me," said Uncle Shawn, a bit nervously. But, even so, he did a Shark Greeting Dance which involved some Undersea Boot hopping, finger wiggling, arm whirling and making a big scared face, then blowing bubbles.

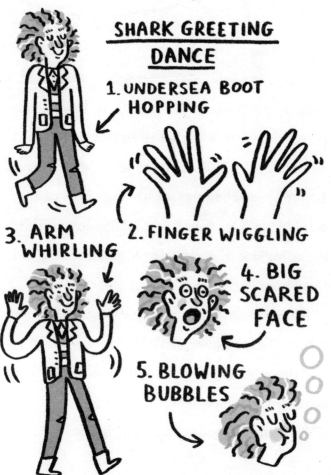

SHARK GREETING DANCE

1. UNDERSEA BOOT HOPPING

2. FINGER WIGGLING

3. ARM WHIRLING

4. BIG SCARED FACE

5. BLOWING BUBBLES

SHARK SIZE DIAGRAM
(TO SCALE)

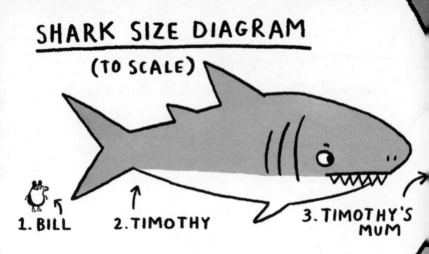

1. BILL   2. TIMOTHY   3. TIMOTHY'S MUM

"Is this them?" asked Timothy's mother in a voice which sounded like cathedrals skiing down gravel. "They look too small to be useful."

"They're small but clever, Mum," said Timothy, nuzzling one of her fins. "All of them would fit in your mouth, but I'd like to swim with the stripy one in my mouth, Mum. Can I? Can I? I like him."

Timothy darted terrifyingly over to Bill and asked, "Do you have a mum?"

"Um, yes. Not quite as big as your mum, but I love her very much."

Timothy wagged all over, which was really a bit

horrifying, even though
he was very nice. He stopped and
said to his mother, "Pleeease." Then he asked Bill,
"Would you like to climb inside my mouth?" He
smiled. "I promise I won't eat you by accident."

Bill swallowed and felt his eyes get really wide.
"Ah, I suppose I might." His legs were trembling
like trousers in a tumble dryer.

"All right. You can have the stripy one and I
will carry everyone else." Timothy's mum nodded.

Before Sam and Sky climbed into the mother
shark's massive cavern of a mouth, they went and
hugged Bill. Then Uncle Shawn came and gave

his best friend the biggest hug he could and whispered, "Riding along in a shark's mouth, all by yourself, like a great badger explorer, or the captain of a shark ship. Won't that be a wonderful adventure?"

This made Bill feel tingly with excitement. No other badger had ever ridden in a shark's mouth! Maybe he really was becoming a Great Badger Explorer!

Bill squeezed Uncle Shawn extra tight, then tilted his ears at a seafaring angle and began to clamber – very carefully – over the dreadful points of Timothy's teeth.

TIMOTHY'S TEETH

"Go to the left where I lost a tooth – you can wriggle through there easily," said Timothy, talking carefully, so as not to knock Bill over.

And then Bill was inside the slippery big whitish and pinkish cave of the shark's mouth.

"Try to keep away from my gill slits – they get a bit whooshy," murmured Timothy gently.

"Sprinkle some powdered air in a corner and it'll make a nice bubble for you to sit in," suggested Uncle Shawn, before he and Sam and Sky tiptoed into the mother shark's mouth.

When everyone was on-board safely, the two great fish gently closed their jaws and the mother shark began to swim, her huge muscles and the dark, high sail of her tail pushing her faster than any human ship. And Timothy thrashed his tail as powerfully as he could, surfing along behind her.

Inside the shark Uncle Shawn was thinking, "Now I have run out of plan... I wonder what will happen next? I bet it will be exciting." He leaned back and ran his fingers through his wibbly hair and smiled. 🐾

BRIAN

FAKE BRIAN

SECTION FIFTEEN

In which there are just too many Brians.

Back on the llama farm there were a lot more llamas. Or, at least, a lot more Brian Llamas.

Everyone had a very strange breakfast. Sitting at the farmhouse table was our pal Brian with his sweet eyes and his lovely kind heart and his wibbly knees. He was just staring at his porridge and looking sad. Carlos, Guinevere and Ginalolobrigida were all staring at the three other Brians round the table. And they were staring at all the other Brians packed into the kitchen and glowering through the windows, and lurking under the table. The other llamas' eyes weren't sweet – they shone purple in a way that looked sore and also nasty.

It was all very worrying.

"How did you do this, Brian?" asked Carlos, too scared to even try making pancakes.

"DO WHAT?" asked far too many Brian voices while the real Brian just looked as if he was going to cry.

"Yes, Brian, did you write asking all your relatives to stay? They look exactly like you," asked Guinevere.

"They are not, excuse me, relatives, they are Brians!" sighed Brian.

"WE LOVE BRIAN!" shouted the Brians.

"Why do they have those purple eyes?" asked Ginalolobrigida. She wanted to pretend she wasn't frightened, but she couldn't help saying, "It is too … scary."

"Never mind that, how did you make them?" asked Carlos.

The real Brian sniffled, "I just please and thank you had a dream about having lots of llama relatives."

"But dreams don't happen in the real world, not like this," snapped Carlos.

Brian sighed again. "I know this very extremely well and yet here are all these so many Brians." His ears drooped. He hadn't eaten any of his porridge because he felt sick and he didn't think it was fair to blame him for all the Brians.

"This is very ridiculous, Brian," Ginalolobrigida began.

She was interrupted by 785 Brians all saying, **"WHAT IS?"**

"Why did you make hundreds of Brians, when you could have made hundreds of me? I am lovely, elegant and charming. Hundreds of me could

change the world with loveliness."

"Well, I'm good at football," said Carlos. "With hundreds of Carloses, I could make many wonderful teams of llama footballers. Everyone would be happy watching them play."

Guinevere shook her head. "That is a big, fat nonsense thing to say. Hundreds of you would make thousands of burning pancakes. I am clever and also good at football and I am good at dancing, bird watching and adding up – hundreds of me would be the most useful."

This annoyed Carlos and Ginalolobrigida, but before they could start an argument, all the purple-eyed Brians turned to them with eyes shining brighter than they ever had. This made everyone stop speaking – everyone except Brian.

Brian had been feeling sad and guilty, but now

he looked at all these other Brians who said they loved him. Then he looked at his friends who were being so nasty and who thought it was such a bad idea for there to be more Brians and he quietly said, "I think my Brians are my real friends. I think now things will be different, because my Brians will look after me. I think everyone should be very nice to me from now on and maybe, please and thank you, you should do what I say."

All the purple-eyed Brians nodded and smiled odd, hard, glittering smiles. Then they said, **"YES!"** Then they all clicked their hooves and teeth together. **"YES! YES! YES!"**

And far away across the meadows poor Claude the spider was being chased by a herd of mechanical spiders who looked very pokey and spiky and horrible.

Claude wanted to look after Brian, but right now he barely had enough time to look after himself.

Oh, dearie, dearie me! 🐾

EVIL DANCE OF JOY

SECTION SIXTEEN

In which there is the nastiest man on Earth.
He is nastier than Grismelda Twark, the angriest
crossing lady in New York. He is nastier than
Norbert Bonescruncher, the completely furious troll
who lives under the Polmadie Bridge in Glasgow.

Deep in his Supervillain Lair, Sylvester Pearlyclaws was dancing for joy. I am sure that you have guessed that all those nasty Brians and mechanical spiders were his fault.

He had used bits of all the clockwork toys he had stolen and given them nasty life by rubbing them with wicked purplonium.

He was bringing everyone's nightmares to life!

So Judge Norris now had a wardrobe full of mechanical criminals who looked just like all of the nastiest real criminals he had sentenced to many, many years in prison. This was so alarming that he no longer opened his wardrobe door and had been wearing the same shirt and suit for eight days.

JUDGE NORRIS'S
MECHANICAL CRIMINALS

SWAG

OLD MOTHER LOOMIS,
CHEESE FORGER

FINGERS McGRUNTY,
BURGLAR

CAPTAIN SNODDY,
CAPTAIN IMPERSONATOR

And poor Claude the spider was being chased about by clockwork spiders that were nearly as good at swinging and climbing and leaping as he was. He was getting really tired by now – but the spiders kept coming.

And, of course, this meant that poor Brian now had 785 other Brians keeping him company. Pearlyclaws hated all Uncle Shawn's lovely friends and he wanted them to be unhappy. He was so delighted when he watched what happened through the tiny cameras he had placed in the Brians' eyes that he danced and danced. His flattened, soft, floppety feet floundered across the nasty, smelly floor.

But he wasn't completely happy. "If I could just see that stupid fat badger's dreams and turn them into nightmares! And where are those nasty little twins? AND WHERE IS UNCLE SHAWN!!?! Something must be stopping the signals from the purplonium in them from

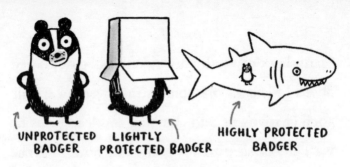

UNPROTECTED BADGER   LIGHTLY PROTECTED BADGER   HIGHLY PROTECTED BADGER

getting through," he growled. He didn't know that Uncle Shawn and Bill and Sky and Sam were protected by being under miles and miles of ocean and being inside two giant sharks. He made himself so angry that he stopped dancing and started trying to tread on the tails of Katie and Bernard the sewer rats. The poor beasts were scampering back and forth out of his way and feeling scared, but also really annoyed.

Bernard whispered, "Oh, I'm fed up of this. Just because we're smelly rats that doesn't mean people shouldn't be nice to us."

Katie whispered back, "I know. And we have lovely whiskers and sparkly eyes..." She was really close to tears.

Bernard frowned as he leaped away from

Pearlyclaws' left foot as it flapped down very close to his ear. "Oh, one day, my dear, we will teach Pearlyclaws a lesson."

"I'm not sure how, because we're only little, but we'll definitely try," agreed Katie.

Then both of them scampered away at top speed and hid behind a huge mound of old chip fat. While they hid, they nibbled bits of it to keep up their strength.

And along the sewer tunnel they could hear Pearlyclaws' voice echoing, "Oooohhh, I will ruin your life, Uncle Shawn. I will ruin all your friends' lives... And then when you are all alone I will squish you under my feet until you are flat and that will take a long time because my feet are all floppety and THAT IS YOUR FAULT." Along the tunnel came the echoing sound of his nose. *"Ffeeep, ffeeep... Ffeeep, ffeeep... Ffeeep, ffeeep... ffee- ee- ee- eep..."*

Oh, dearie, dearie, dearie me. 🐾

SANDWICHES

SECTION SEVENTEEN

*In which – thank goodness – there is Uncle
Shawn and here are Sam and Sky and here
is Badger Bill and they are speeding on their
way to make things better for everyone!*

Inside the mother shark's dark cavern of a mouth,
Uncle Shawn and Sam and Sky were having sandwiches, because it felt like lunchtime. Uncle Shawn
had scattered lots of powdered air about and he
and the twins were sitting in a big safe bubble
while water swirled in and out through the gill slits.
When they shone their torches beyond the air bubble, everything looked a bit like the inside of a huge

washing machine at midnight, only with teeth…

"Excuse me, Mrs Shark, but would you like a sandwich?" asked Uncle Shawn politely. You should always be polite to sharks, especially when they're gigantunormous. "There's jam, or honey, or lemon curd."

"Call me Florence," said the massive shark voice, rumbling around her massive mouth and making everyone's hair stand on end. "One of each, please. It is very hard to get jam or honey under the ocean and I have never tasted lemon curd."

So Uncle Shawn and Sam and Sky gently threw sandwiches down towards Florence's throat.

"Oooohhh, lovely," thundered Florence.

"Our pleasure," said Sky.

Meanwhile, deep dark waters were shooshing and whooshing past the sides of the huge beast. While Sam and Sky sat on Florence's tongue and felt a little bit seasick, she zoomed over telephone cables full of conversations and shipwrecks full of

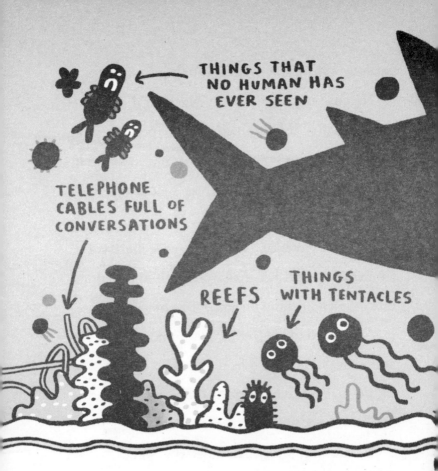

THINGS THAT NO HUMAN HAS EVER SEEN

TELEPHONE CABLES FULL OF CONVERSATIONS

REEFS

THINGS WITH TENTACLES

treasure and reefs and chasms full of things with tentacles and big boggly eyes and things that no human has ever seen.

Uncle Shawn sprinkled a few more handfuls of powdered air onto the floor of Florence's mouth, then sat down and crossed his long legs. He looked

BILL

THINGS WITH BIG BOGGLY EYES

SHIPWRECKS FULL OF TREASURE

CHASMS

puzzled. "I wonder why the Living Fish Tree is so sad and ill? And does this have anything to do with all of the purpleness everywhere? Hmmm... If I did not think Pearlyclaws was locked up safely in prison I would guess he had something to do with so much nastiness... Hmmm..."

Sam said, "He is very good at escaping."

"Indeed he is... Hmmm. I have been too busy to check the news for ages... Maybe he escaped from the courtroom while he was on trial."

Sky said, "We'll have to do something to make the Living Fish Tree better, or all the sea creatures will get sick and everyone on land will have no underpants and will never be able to tell the tiniest fib to anyone, not even to stop their feelings being hurt."

"That is very true." Uncle Shawn nodded.

Florence made everyone's knees jiggle by saying, "The egg case I grew up in was kept safe among the seaweed that grows on the Living Fish Tree's limbs. Now no one can wake her up. We all want her to be well. She loves taking care of young creatures and is very kind."

Uncle Shawn's hair nodded. "She helps people be kind, too, even on land. Whenever humans say nice things that aren't quite true, to cheer up

other humans, she stops our pants exploding. Hmmm... I will have to think about rescuing for a while." Then he leaned his long spine against the soft side of the shark's mouth and closed his eyes and seemed to go to sleep.

So Sky and Sam took out the cards that Uncle Shawn had put into their backpacks in case there were times when they had a break from being adventurous and they played snap on Florence's tongue. Every now and then Florence would softly rumble, "Mmmm. Tickly."

While they played, Sam said, "I bet Sylvester Pearlyclaws is behind all this. Anything this wicked would be just what he would enjoy."

Sky nodded. "He probably escaped and is hiding somewhere. I wonder if there's a way we could find out where..."

"That should be part of our plan." Sam nodded. "And we have to help Uncle Shawn make the Living Fish Tree better. But I don't know what kind of medicine a giant magical octopus would need."

"Maybe she is bored and we ought to teach her some games?" suggested Sky.

"Or maybe she should start painting pictures? With eight arms she would be a wonderful painter!" said Sam.

"Maybe she is tired out from being kind and needs to get some kindness back!"

Uncle Shawn smiled and listened. The clever twins were helping him think of his plan...

Meanwhile Florence was taking her favourite route away from Scotland and then across the Atlantic to the Panama Canal. The Panama Canal is very big. Huge cargo ships and ocean liners use it to cross from the Atlantic to the Pacific Ocean.

Florence had to breathe in all the way through

the canal, because it was a very tight fit for a fish as gigantunormous as her. Nobody noticed her, apart from a small boy called Derian who was sitting near the Pacific end of the canal and inventing new types of rocket ship in his head for fun. He happened to glance over just as Florence emerged from the canal into the ocean by leaping over the lock gates. She was a terrifying and magnificent sight, with the sun gleaming off her gorgeous grey sides. Derian knew no one would believe him if he told them about it. But he smiled for weeks afterwards and started to draw plans for a shark-shaped rocket...

Inside Florence, Sam and Sky and Uncle Shawn all felt their tummies go flippety flop as she leaped and they watched sunshine appear between her teeth. Then they all felt the enormous SPLOOSH as she landed back in the water and dived down again.

Swimming bravely right behind Florence came her son, Timothy, who was only as big as a pile of buses. He wasn't used to going so very far and very fast.

"Ooofff. I don't know if I can keep this up," Timothy said carefully, so that Bill wouldn't get bounced around too much. Bill was starting to really enjoy the rush of water everywhere and the sound of the undersea creatures speaking and the whales singing to each other. He had already eaten all his sandwiches by the light of his little torch. He was having an adventure and adventures make you hungry.

"Mum is one of the fastest sharks in the whole wet world. Oooohhh, my tail's sore," complained Timothy.

"You're doing very well!" called Bill. "You're the bravest shark I've met."

"Oh, that's so nice of you." Timothy sighed. "I sometimes think nobody likes sharks at all.

You're the nicest badger I've met."

"Have you met lots of badgers?"

"Well, no. I haven't met any. But if I ever do see another little furry and stripy landbeast I won't even think about eating it all up in one mouthful."

"Um… That's nice," said Bill, getting goosebumps.

"Ouch!" said Timothy as he banged his nose on the lock gates. He didn't know how he would get past them. "These are so high and strong and Mum must have just jumped over them. But I'm not sure if I can – they seem very tall… Oh…"

Bill knew what it was like to be worried you might not be able to do something difficult so he told Timothy, "I bet a big fast shark like you will be really good at leaping over things."

"I don't know…"

"Swim back a bit, speed up and then pretend you're a great big grey eagle."

"Well…"

"You'll do it."

"Well… If you think I can…"

"You can do it! You can do it!"

With Bill cheering him on the brave, enormous shark swam back, shook his fins and then … swam as fast as he could and then a bit faster towards the gates and then…

Ooooohhhhh…

Bill's stomach went flippety, floopety, like a jelly falling down stairs, as Timothy rushed out of the water, into the air and RIGHT OVER THE LOCK GATES!

HOORAY!

"Well done! Ow!" The big thump when Timothy landed made Bill somersault all round the shark's mouth, but now they were in the Pacific and much closer to rescuing the Living Fish Tree!

"Have you ever seen the Living Fish Tree?" asked Bill.

"Only when I was a baby. My mum left my egg case there. I was born on Limb Number 5, next to some starfish. Looking at the Living Fish Tree made you feel nice all through and no fishermen's nets or hooks ever came near her. She was so kind. But when I grew up I swam away and never went back to visit her. Maybe none of the creatures who grow up in her arms go back; that would be very sad. I wonder if we're making her ill..." Timothy sighed.

And far away, in the middle of the Pacific, the Living Fish Tree glowed more and more faintly and the waters got more and more purple and Sophie the albatross got more and more weak.

Oh no! 🐾

SECTION EIGHTEEN

In which there are lots of purple eyes, lots

of hooves and eight worried legs.

The following morning, back at Uncle Shawn's llama farm, things had gone from strange to worse.

While Brian had slept incredibly well, guarded by dozens of purple-eyed Brians, Claude the spider had escaped the mechanical spiders and now tip-toed along beams and swung on spiderweb ropes across what were, for him, huge spaces. Finally, he landed gently on the head of one of the purple-eyed llamas. Under his feet the llama felt all hard and lumpy and his sensitive spider ears could hear ticking and clicking noises and whirring…

"Dearie me," thought our spider pal. "These are clockwork llamas, not soft, lovely real llamas. I don't think Brian is safe with them…"

Claude swung and dropped and crept along to where Brian was sleeping soundly in his bed of straw. Claude tap-danced along Brian's sensitive nose until the llama woke up.

"Waah. Oh, Señor Claude. You have woken me…"

Claude waved half his legs in the air and shouted in his loudest, but still teeny, spider voice, "YOU ARE NOT SAFE, MY FRIEND. THESE ARE NOT REAL LLAMAS."

But as soon as Claude spoke all the purple-eyed Brians turned to stare at him. The nasty glow of their eyes started to make his tiny spider body very hot.

"These are all my new friends," said Brian.

"YES! WE ARE BRIAN'S FRIENDS!" said all the purple-eyed llamas.

"They're nice," mumbled Brian, going back to sleep.

"BEGONE ENEMY OF BRIANS! WE ARE THE BRIAN FRIEND ARMY!"

All the purple-eyed Brians stared even harder at poor little Claude.

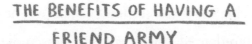

THE BENEFITS OF HAVING A FRIEND ARMY

THEY ALWAYS LET YOU WIN AT GAMES

MANY BIRTHDAY PRESENTS

LOTS OF LLAMAS TO BLOW ON YOUR CUSTARD IF IT'S TOO HOT

ALWAYS A LLAMA TO HELP YOU LIFT HEAVY THINGS

VERY BIG CUDDLES

The staring from the purple eyes was making Claude's poor feet frizzle and his back burn, so he swung on his spider silk and ran up into the dark corners of the barn's roof to hide away for a while and think.

As he climbed one of his favourite beams, he said to himself in his tiny spider voice, "I need a plan to rescue poor Brian. Even if he is being very silly."

Down in his straw bed Brian started to have a strange dream about clockwork evil llamas. It was such an odd dream that it woke him up.

As soon as Brian opened his eyes, all of the purple-eyed Brians said, **"ALL HAIL TO THE GREAT BRIAN! WE WILL DEFEND YOU BETTER THAN ANY SPIDER! WE WILL MAKE ALL CREATURES AND LLAMAS OBEY YOU! HOORAY FOR KING BRIAN!"**

"Oh, Señors, I am not sure about that, you know…" said Brian, feeling embarrassed.

"HAIL BRIAN! NO LLAMAS LOVE

YOU AS MUCH AS WE LOVE YOU!"

And some of the purple-eyed Brians lifted him onto their backs and carried him, while the rest cheered and trotted alongside.

"YOU WILL NEVER HAVE TO WALK AGAIN!"

"But, honourable Señors, I like walking," explained Brian as he was bounced along by the galloping llamas.

"HAIL BRIAN! HOORAY!"

So Brian just decided to let them carry him, because it did feel quite nice. Maybe they did love him more than anyone…

Claude watched the llamas go and then began twanging a message on the special thread that connected him to The World Association of Spiders. This was called the World Wide Web and was very useful.

"Poor Brian. I do hope you'll be okay," whispered Claude, waving one of his legs sadly, as Brian went out of sight. "I do hope all the other spiders aren't having Purple Problems that will stop them helping…" sighed Claude.

But in every corner and shadow and curtain and bathroom the spiders of the world were having terrible trouble as the purpleness slowed down their tiny legs. No spider help was going to arrive this time. Oh no! 🐾

THE DARKEST, DEEPEST AND MOST SECRET DEPTHS OF THE PACIFIC OCEAN

SECTION NINETEEN

In which there is a wonderful uncle

who is good at rescuing. Hooray!

The two gigantunormous sharks had finally reached the darkest, deepest and most secret depths of the Pacific Ocean, where they knew the Living Fish Tree made her home.

Inside Florence Shark, Uncle Shawn and Sam and Sky felt their racing progress slow to a gently bobbing drift. They watched as Florence opened her enormous jaws and a faint, sad, wibbly under-water light crept in.

Carefully, Uncle Shawn climbed over Florence's

teeth and then helped the twins to climb out onto the ocean floor. Towering above them was the wonderful Living Fish Tree – the most wise and kind and magical, gigantunormous octopus in the world. Some of her long arms still reached up through miles and miles of ocean, almost to the surface, but they were very still. Others just lay on the sand of the seabed.

"Oh, she is so beautiful!" Uncle Shawn smiled

sadly. "But she looks so poorly." He walked towards her and stroked one of her legs gently and watched as little sparks of rainbow light spread upwards and then faded. "Hmmmm... A little bit of kindness makes her a little bit better. But we will need such a lot of kindness to cure such a huge and wonderful creature... Hmmm...

"Thank you so much, Florence," said Uncle Shawn, reaching up to pat the massive shark's nose very, very gently.

"Yes, thanks," said Sam.

"That was the most exciting journey we've ever had!" said Sky. "Including going to the moon!"

Florence grinned with all of her teeth and everyone made sure not to scream.

"Hmmm..." bubbled Uncle Shawn, looking into the distance. This made everyone peer at the misty blue ocean depths. There were swimming shapes out there, circling and circling... And they looked like – EVEN MORE SHARKS!

DOZENS OF SHARKS!

"Oh, no," said Sam.

Sky added, "I'm not sure all sharks are as nice as Timothy and Florence."

But Florence just grinned even wider. "These are all of my Extremely Great White Shark relations. They were all born in the arms of the Living Fish Tree and they have come back to guard her."

The Living Fish Tree's eyes were closed and her skin was almost all grey. Before the twins could swim any closer to her, Timothy Shark arrived – very out of breath. Bill tumbled out of his huge mouth in a cloud of bubbles.

"Mum, Mum," shouted Timothy. "I jumped over those lock gates in one go, didn't I Bill? Bill is my best friend ever."

Timothy nudged Bill fondly with the broad tip of his nose and sent the badger tumbling through the water until he landed on his back, looking straight up into the arms of the octopus everyone called the

VERY HORRIFYING EXTREMELY GREAT WHITE SHARKS DOING FRIENDLY THINGS

JEFFREY KNITTING

ANGELA WAVING

BETSY PLAYING THE ACCORDION

DEBORAH DANCING

Living Fish Tree. "Woo. Waagh," Bill bubbled.

"Careful, Timothy." Florence frowned. "But well done for so much brave swimming and excellent jumping."

Uncle Shawn ran his watery fingers through his watery hair. "I have a feeling that some other creature is in trouble, too. Hmmm…"

Bill looked up and saw a teeny, tiny dark dot that seemed to be floating on the surface of the

water. "What do you think that is, Uncle Shawn?"

Uncle Shawn took his folding telescope out of his pocket and looked up. There he could see a small, sad shape surrounded by evil-looking purple clouds. It seemed to have a beak…

"Oh, well done, Bill! This is exactly who we need to help first – and we need to be very fast!" Uncle Shawn turned to Timothy. "Young Timothy, it would take me a terribly long time to swim all the way up there. Do you think you would be able to lift me to the surface and help me do something kind?"

Timothy wagged his tail even harder and the limbs of the octopus waved a tiny bit. (And the octopus's magical eyes flickered open just for a moment.)

Bill took Uncle Shawn's hand and smiled up at him, just the way that an adventurous badger explorer might. "Uncle Shawn, do you think…"

Uncle Shawn grinned his biggest grin. "Of course, I really couldn't do something this exciting without my best friend."

Timothy grinned horrifyingly. "Bill is my friend, too. He is a famous badger explorer."

"Well, nearly." Bill blushed.

"All right, then. Sam and Sky, while I am away I would like you to hug your arms as far as you

181

can around an octopus arm each and while you do, tell it kind things. If I'm right, I think that might make her a little bit better, while we get ready for the next part of the plan." Then Uncle Shawn turned to Bill and his blue eyes shone. "No badger has ever ridden on a shark all the way from the bottom of the Pacific Ocean to the top. Are you ready?"

"Oh, yes! Hooray!" shouted Bill, in an extra-big cloud of bubbles.

"I think, though..." Timothy blushed and mumbled. "Maybe you should balance on my nose as I swim upwards and then you will be the first thing anyone catches sight of. I can just stay underneath the waves, in case anyone might be scared of me."

Bill nodded. "Even though you are a very friendly shark."

"Yes, perhaps that would be sensible," said Uncle Shawn.

So Timothy held himself very steady and let Uncle Shawn and Bill climb up onto his nose. Then he swam as fast – but as gently – as he could with his head going straight up and his tail pointing all the way down.

"Wheeeeee!" called Bill and Uncle Shawn, putting their arms out for balance. Up they went, faster than any rocket, towards the surface of the water. A brave badger and a brave uncle, riding an Extremely Great White Shark – it was quite a sight!

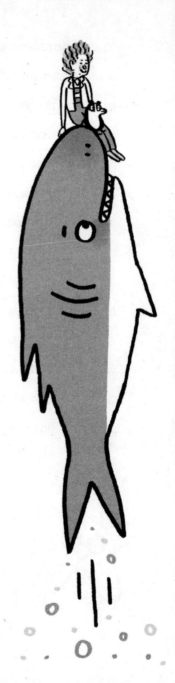

As they went up, the water was getting lighter and lighter and the tiny dot up above them was growing larger and beginning to look like a tangled mass of nasty, purple, glowing wool.

And who do we know who is stuck in the middle of the Pacific Ocean with their lovely webbed albatross feet stuck in nasty, purple, glowing wool?

Yes! It was Sophie the albatross! And she needed rescuing!

Uncle Shawn and Bill zoomed up out of the water – SPABLOOSH – and nearly flew straight off the end of Timothy's nose. They both had to waggle their arms like starfish at a disco, just to

stop themselves falling over.

"Mmmm?" croaked a tired, dry, little voice. Sophie was so thirsty and hungry and exhausted by now that she couldn't even manage to be surprised when a tall, skinny man with wibbly hair and a badger suddenly appeared beside her in the middle of the Pacific Ocean, apparently standing on a bouncy grey island.

"Hello, young albatross," said Uncle Shawn softly.

"We're here to help," whispered Bill. He knew how horrible it was to be small and scared and waiting for someone kind to rescue you.

"You seem to be all tangled up," said Uncle

Shawn, waggling his long clever fingers. "It's lucky that I am the Pandrumdroochit Wool Untangling Champion."

Sophie thought she must be dreaming as Uncle Shawn's friendly face leaned in towards her and he started to gently tug at the nasty wool. A big tear of joy rolled down her large and wonderful beak. "Have you really, really come to help me?"

"Of course," said Uncle Shawn and winked.

"I've been here for ages and ages and ages and I was feeling so lonely and..." Sophie's brave beak was trembling.

Bill reached into his backpack and got out his Big Badger Supply Company thermos and matching cup. He filled the cup with nice fresh lemonade and then fed her little bits of his very last biscuit.

"Oh, thank you. I'm Sophie," she whispered.

"I am Uncle Shawn and I'm here to help. And this is my best friend Bill."

Bill smiled and started to help untangle the wool, putting every piece they pulled away into his backpack so it couldn't tangle anyone else. "What a marvellous beak you have – and what lovely wings."

"Thank you," murmured Sophie. "And you have wonderful stripes." She peered at Uncle Shawn with her tired eyes. "Are you the Uncle Shawn who helps animals? My mum and dad told me about you."

Uncle Shawn just smiled and kept on untangling the wool.

He had noticed that every bit of wool he and Bill touched stopped being purple. For a moment the wool would be covered with a sparkling rainbow-coloured shimmer and then it went back to its real colours and seemed to be just ordinary wool. This made him think. "Hmmm... The purple doesn't like us being kind to Sophie. When we touch the wool, the purple goes away and looks much friendlier..."

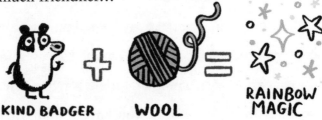

KIND BADGER + WOOL = RAINBOW MAGIC

The more wool they touched, the more rainbow glittering happened and the less purple there was. Little patches of purple in the sea even started to fade all by themselves, turning sparkly and then disappearing. Even a small purple cloud drifting overhead glimmered with magical light and then became just a normal white fluffy cloud.

"Hmmm..." said Uncle Shawn. "All the purple seems to be connected, somehow. What happens to one bit, happens to other bits, even without them touching." He rubbed his wibbly hair to make his brain work a bit faster. "So it is a clever, nasty purple thing." He crinkled his nose for extra wisdom. "Yes! There is only one thing I know that is purple and clever and nasty and killed by kindness – purplonium!"

"I thought no one knew where the purplonium had been hidden?" asked Bill.

"But I have a horrible feeling Pearlyclaws found out." Uncle Shawn frowned. "No one else would be wicked enough to search for the wickedest thing on Earth and then use it to make everyone miserable!"

The two friends kept untangling the wool and watching it change into something more friendly.

NASTY KNOTS

DOUBLE ELBOWED KNOT   **RUNNING LLAMA KNOT**   **QUADRUPLE AUNT KNOT**

CORAL REEF KNOT   **PEG LEG KNOT**

SELF-TYING FOUR WAY CONFUSION   **FOUR STRAND PARROT HITCH**   **SHAG MANGLE TANGLE**

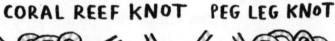

STRAIGHT INVISIBLE KNOT

Finally, there was just one nasty knot of wool left, keeping Sophie trapped. It wriggled and glowed with a bright, hard purple light. No matter what they tried, Uncle Shawn and Bill couldn't break it or move it to free poor Sophie!

"I wish I had brought some scissors," sighed Uncle Shawn, stroking Sophie's beak.

"I know someone better than scissors," said Bill. "And so do you!"

Uncle Shawn smiled. "Yes! Timothy's teeth!" He asked Sophie, "My dear young albatross, can I ask a friend to help us?"

"You have a friend with you?"

"I am standing on his nose."

"Oh, dear. He must be very big..."

"Gigantunormous. But also very kind and polite. I promise you will be safe."

So Uncle Shawn and Bill jumped off the end of Timothy's nose and bobbed about in the ocean while Timothy lifted his head – and his mouth – all the way out of the water...

"Eeep!"

He winked at Sophie. "Excuse me." Then he very gently used the edge of his tiniest tooth to just – *shnick* – snip the wool and free Sophie.

When Sophie felt her leg pull free she couldn't help smiling, even though Timothy did seem terrifying. "Thank you!"

"My pleasure. I'm Timothy, a very, very friendly shark," he said in his quietest voice, which still ruffled all Sophie's feathers.

"You're quite safe now," said Uncle Shawn.

Sophie looked into Uncle Shawn's twinkly blue eyes. Then she wriggled her legs and paddled her feet and stretched out her beautiful wings. She was free! All over!

Then Uncle Shawn gave Sophie all the sandwiches he had left, to get her strength up.

"Thank you so much, Uncle Shawn. And thank you stripy Bill. And thank you big shark."

After that Sophie began her long, long run across the surface of the water. Would she still be strong enough to fly? Would

192

she be all right? Everyone watched to find out.

She stretched her vast wings as wide as they could go. On and on she went until – YES! – she was soaring beautifully upwards and laughing and calling out! "Oh, it's so wonderful to fly again! Oh, how very nice to have air tickling under my wings. Goodbye! Goodbye! Goodbye!"

Uncle Shawn and Timothy watched her go and Bill waved until his arm was sore.

"I'm not crying," said Timothy. "I just have salty water in my eyes."

Of course, Timothy really was crying, so he was telling a bit of a fib. That meant that a large bubble of purple whooshed out into the water around Timothy's bottom. "Oooohhh. I do beg your pardon." Then he added, "She was so nice. And she's so good at flying."

Uncle Shawn hugged his arms around one of

Timothy's fins. (He could just about reach.) And Bill hugged Timothy and Uncle Shawn and all of their love and friendliness made Timothy's purple cloud in the water sparkle and then disappear. Bill smiled and waved once more at the tiny pale shape that was Sophie, far away.

"And now the Living Fish Tree needs us," said Uncle Shawn. "And I have a plan." He wiggled his long, wet fingers through his long wet hair. "At least I think I have a plan..." He winked.

Then Bill and Uncle Shawn took a quick handful of powdered air each, climbed onto Timothy's back and plunged back down towards the faintly glowing giant octopus known as the Living Fish Tree. They had more work to do! 🐾

KING BRIAN

SECTION TWENTY

In which there is lots of purple wickedness! Oh, no!

Meanwhile, Brian was being carried round and round the farm, balanced on the purple-eyed Brians. Brian was feeling that maybe he might be more important than he'd thought.

It is very easy to feel like a king if you are being carried about like a king and hundreds of purple-eyed llamas are shouting, **"HAIL BRIAN! LONG LIVE KING BRIAN! HAIL BRIAN! MAY HE RULE FOR EVER!"**

Brian felt prouder by the minute. "Thank you. Please and thank you I could perhaps be

King Brian." He was about to try waving royally when Ginalolobrigida appeared round a corner, trotting daintily beside an incredibly handsome llama.

"¡*Hola!*" called Ginalolobrigida.

"Why are you not bowing to me?" asked Brian, trying to act like a llama king.

"Do not be so foolish, you foolish big llama fool. I am here with Alfonso Aparador, a llama who is much more wonderful than you in every way," shouted Ginalolobrigida Llama. She was wearing pink and green eyeshadow and purple lipstick. Alfonso had suggested she ought to in his grating, clockwork-sounding voice. She thought the new colour scheme looked horrible, but she didn't feel she could contradict Alfonso.

Of course, you will have guessed this wasn't Alfonso – it was a nasty clockwork robot giving nasty fashion advice and controlled by nasty Pearlyclaws.

Alfonso Aparador glared at Brian with bright purple eyes. Just as Brian's fur was starting to feel a bit hot, Guinevere raced out from behind the llama barns pursued by hundreds of wiggly pink hippos. This would have been very sweet if they hadn't had snapping metal jaws and bright purple eyes.

"Brian! Help me!" she yelled as she galloped past. "Gina! Why don't you and your boyfriend help me?"

But before anyone could help her, here came Carlos Llama who was spitting at someone who looked just like Capitán Fantástico Llama – except that Capitán Fantástico didn't have glimmering purple eyes and was only supposed to be in comic books...

Oh, dearie, dearie, dearie, dearie me!

What could possibly happen next?

EMERGENCIA!

The only person who knew what would happen next was sitting in his smelly Supervillain Lair, watching his monitors and twiddling with the dials and switches on rows of remote control boxes, sending commands to all the dreadful mechanical creatures he had built and brought to nasty life with purplonium. He couldn't wait to upset Uncle Shawn's llama friends more and more. "If only I could find that stupid fat badger and horrible, horrible Uncle Shawn. They must be somewhere very far from the farm..."

Still, Pearlyclaws was happy that all over the world, everyone's nightmares were coming to life! And there were almost no unexploded underpants anywhere! And the sky had been getting more and more purple. Sylvester Pearlyclaws now kept Katie and Bernard the sewer rats awake every night with his dancing and singing in nastily wicked joy. His nose joined in with *ffeeep ffeeep* noises and this made Katie's whiskers ache.

While Bill and Uncle Shawn were riding upwards on Timothy's nose, Pearlyclaws had been enjoying his wickedness so much that he started to feel peckish. This meant that he was in his Kitchenette of Wickedness making nasty smelly toast while Uncle Shawn rescued Sophie and began to work out how to stop the purplonium. Pearlyclaws didn't notice his big jar of purplonium shine a bit less brightly... 🐾

SECTION TWENTY-ONE

In which there is a very poorly octopus – and lots of

people and creatures who are trying to help her...

Underneath the Pacific Ocean, our friends were trying to make a Living Fish Tree Wake Up And Feel Better Plan.

Uncle Shawn remembered, "Sam and Sky, while we were in Florence's mouth, you had very good ideas about how to make the Living Fish Tree feel well again."

Sam said, "Like being nice to her!"

"And bringing her interesting things?" asked Sky.

"People being nice to me and interesting things always make me feel better," said Bill. "And maybe some nice soup when I can sit up and drink it."

"Yes!" said Uncle Shawn and waggled his arms like an underwater conductor. "So let's all be interesting and nice and fun. Dear shark friends, can you be extra-specially nice and fun and interesting for the Living Fish Tree, please?"

Timothy and his mum whispered to each other in low rumbles that shook the sand. Then Florence started to spin on her tail like the hugest ballerina ever. Timothy grinned and swam loop-the-loops round his mum, blew bubbles and rolled over and over until he felt a bit sick. It was all very impressive and everyone clapped and cheered. But it did almost no good. The poorly octopus only raised one eyelid a tiny bit.

Sam and Sky went back to hugging their arms as far as they could around her huge limbs and sang "Badger Boogie Blues" while Bill shimmied and shoomied across the sand in his stone boots. This made both the Living Fish Tree's eyelids lift for a moment, but that was all.

Bill sat next to the giant octopus and told her the best badger stories he knew. He recited The Tale of The Tail, a story about a small badger whose tail is stolen by a goblin and replaced with a stick of peppermint rock.

Then he told her about Bumpertook the Brave, the story of a nervous young badger who has hundreds of adventures and saves thousands of animals and humans and then retires to a tiny village and grows carrots. This made the octopus's eyes open all the way and then stay open.

Then Uncle Shawn danced every single one of his dances – The Albatross Joy Dance, The Honey Bee Direction Deciding Dance, The Wall Crumbling Dance, The Smock and Clog Dance, The Summoning Dance and the Get Well Soon Dance. Bill, Sam, Sky, Timothy and Florence all joined in with the Get Well Soon Dance and you can imagine how impressive that was with so many arms and legs and fins wiggling and jiggling in the water.

The poorly octopus watched all this with her big clever eyes and her whole body did shine a tiny bit more brightly for a few minutes. But then the light faded. She wasn't strong.

"Dearie, dearie," bubbled Uncle Shawn. "Until we get rid of all this purple purplonium I don't think she can really get well. And that means we need to find out for sure who is behind all this. We need to know if Pearlyclaws is using purplonium to hurt everyone. Hmmm..."

Bill scratched his whiskers to make himself feel cleverer. "Uncle Shawn? If one bit of purplonium can talk to another bit of purplonium..."

"And maybe Pearlyclaws is talking to all the purplonium," interrupted Sky. "Like a great big purple evil internet..."

"Then we might be able..." interrupted Sam.

"To use the purplonium to reach all the way to Pearlyclaws!" finished Bill.

Uncle Shawn grinned one of his biggest grins. "I have such clever friends." Uncle Shawn turned to Bill. "I have an idea. What if we took all the wool you have in your backpack that used to be nasty and covered in purplonium? Now that it's nice, maybe it will help us."

So Bill took out the wool and Sam and Sky and Bill tried holding it, but nothing happened.

"Well, maybe we have to make the wool purple again..." said Uncle Shawn.

"That could be dangerous," said Bill.

"But I'm with my friends and you'll help me if anything goes wrong." Uncle Shawn nodded to Bill and the twins.

"Are you sure, Uncle Shawn?"

Uncle Shawn nodded, being brave. "Yes, Bill. Now we need some purple..."

Before Uncle Shawn could say anything else, Timothy yelled, "I'm a bicycle!"

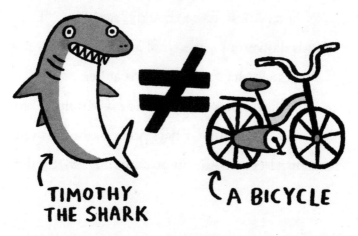

TIMOTHY
THE SHARK

A BICYCLE

Of course, this wasn't true. Timothy had far too many teeth to be a bicycle. So purple cloud appeared all around his shark bottom.

Uncle Shawn quickly waved the wool in the purple cloud and slowly it started to shine and glimmer wickedly. "It's working! Oh, and it's stinging my fingers!"

"Careful, Uncle Shawn!" shouted Bill.

Uncle Shawn lifted the wool up to his ear. "I can sort of almost nearly hear something – like lots of evil ants chatting." But then he shook his head. "It's no good, though. I can't hear enough. You will have to wrap my head in the evil wool," said Uncle Shawn, trying to smile.

"I don't know if we should," said Sky. "That sounds dangerous – the wool is really nasty."

But Uncle Shawn just winked at her.

So Bill and Sam and Sky slowly wrapped the wicked wool around Uncle Shawn's head, even though it seemed to nip at their fingers. By the time they had finished, all they could see of him was a big purple ball of wool with Uncle Shawn's wibbly hair waving out of the top.

WIBBLY HAIR

WOOL

"Mmmmmffmm," said Uncle Shawn. And Bill pulled some of the wool back so that Uncle Shawn could speak.

"It's working! I am beginning to hear buzzes and whispers and bits of words! The wool is letting me listen to the Purple Internet! And I can hear a name. I can hear it over and over – Curlydrawers? Burlyfloors?"

"PEARLYCLAWS!" shouted Bill and Sam and Sky.

"Stop now before you get hurt!" called Bill.

But Uncle Shawn was trying to listen deeper and deeper into the Purple Internet.

GREAT BIG PURPLE EVIL INTERNET

UNCLE SHAWN

THE FARM

Uncle Shawn heard jumbles of words: **hate them... hurt them... tangle the fish...**

It all made him feel trembly inside, it was so nasty. And then he heard something even worse than that!

**KEEP TELLING BRIAN
HE IS YOUR KING!**

KEEP CHASING GUINEVERE!

KEEP FRIGHTENING CARLOS!

KEEP UPSETTING GINALOLOBRIGIDA!

KEEP SCARING CLAUDE!

**AND KEEP LOOKING FOR THAT
STUPID FAT BADGER BILL AND
THAT STUPID HAPPY UNCLE!**

HATE UNCLE SHAWN!

FIND UNCLE SHAWN!

HUNT HIM DOWN AND HATE HIM!

Of course, it was very horrible to hear any of this, but it was even worse because Uncle Shawn recognised the names of his llama pals and his best friend! And, even worse, he recognised the voice sending out all these horrible commands – it really was Sylvester Wilberforce Humbertly Pearlyclaws and he had control of purplonium, the most purple and wicked thing ever!

Almost as soon as Uncle Shawn had got far enough along the Purple Internet to hear Pearlyclaws' voice, the wool around his head began to get hot – and then it began to get tight. The purplonium had found him – it knew he was there!

"Oh, no!" yelped Bill. "Look – the wool is starting to smother Uncle Shawn!"

"Quick!" Bill, Sky and Sam rushed forward and started to pull at the strands as the wool tightened around Uncle Shawn's ears and his face until they were really sore.

"Mmmmhmmnnn!" Uncle Shawn tried to yell as Pearlyclaws' evil orders tugged strands of wool over his mouth again.

By now the wool was shining bright purple and hurting Uncle Shawn. He was feeling faint. The twins and Uncle Shawn's best badger pal tried to get their fingers under the strands of wool, but the purplonium was too strong.

Timothy swam in and tried to nip at the threads with his teeth and Florence joined him, but every strand the huge sharks snipped just grew back together again.

SHARK TOOTH

STRONG   STRONGER   UNBELIEVABLY STRONG

Oh, no!

EMERGENCIA!!

They couldn't rescue Uncle Shawn!

Everything looked hopeless. As Uncle Shawn fell to the sandy seabed, the huge octopus arms began to twitch and shiver. Then the octopus's skin began to shimmer and glisten with faint rainbow light. And then one of the Living Fish Tree's clever and incredibly strong arms swooshed along the seabed, faster than Florence Shark chasing her dinner.

With his very last strength and breath, Uncle Shawn thought as hard as he could, "Don't listen to Pearlyclaws! I am coming to deal with you Pearlyclaws! Kindness is coming!" This weakened the purplonium so much that the octopus's powerful arm and suckers could tug and tear at the wool and – finally! – pulled it off like a nasty balaclava.

Phew!

The purple wool glowed with bright rainbow colours and floated up high above them like a little moon.

UNBELIEVABLY STRONG

STRONGER THAN EVERYTHING ELSE

Uncle Shawn and octopus magic were stronger than purplonium!

Everyone cheered.

"Thank you, Living Fish Tree. Thank you so much." Uncle Shawn sat up and ate extra handfuls of powdered air.

Everyone hugged everyone for a very long time and Bill's eyes went all misty. "Uncle Shawn, I'm so glad you're better."

But the effort of saving Uncle Shawn had really

tired the wonderful octopus. Our pals had helped to make her feel a tiny bit better, but now her eyes had closed again. All her arms drifted helplessly and her skin turned back to a sad grey.

Bill said to Uncle Shawn, "I'm so glad you're safe. But look at the poor Living Fish Tree!"

Uncle Shawn held Bill's hand. "I'm glad I'm safe too." Uncle Shawn sighed. "We gave the Living Fish Tree a little bit of strength, but it wasn't enough. She is exhausted now. So we really have to go and defeat Pearlyclaws. I think the llamas are in terrible trouble, too. We need to go home! But there's one more thing we need to do. And I will need everyone to help me!"

Uncle Shawn, Bill, Sky, Sam, Timothy and Florence all held hands and fins in a circle and then they started on the next part of Uncle Shawn's plan... 🐾

VERY HOT
PURPLE
EYES

SECTION TWENTY-TWO

In which we find out exactly what is happening
back at the llama farm and – oh dearie me! – Uncle
Shawn was right! The llamas are in terrible trouble!

And meanwhile everything on the llama farm
was very horrible and confusing.

Capitán Fantástico chased poor Carlos into
Brian's llama barn. Guinevere raced into the
barn after him, just ahead of the purple-eyed
miniature hippos. And right behind them came
Ginalolobrigida Llama, chased by Alfonso
Aparador. Carlos and Ginalolobrigida helped
Guinevere bar the door and push hay bales

against it but our llama pals could hear the hippos' nasty metal jaws starting to nibble at the wood.

And, high above them in the rafters, Claude was shouting, "OH DEAR! THIS IS TERRIBLE!" in his tiny spider voice.

Up in the rafters very tiny fires were starting everywhere as mechanical spider eyes stared at the wooden beams and made them burn. Poor Claude!

"What is happening? Dreams are not supposed to happen when you are awake!" shouted Carlos. "I do not like Capitán Fantástico any more, not one bit!"

"And they are not supposed to chase you!" shouted Guinevere. "I wish Uncle Shawn was here! He'd know what to do!"

Outside purple-eyed Alfonso Aparador was starting to recite some of the most horrible poetry the world had ever heard.

I love the smell of llama poo,
I'd like to put it in a stew.
Ooty-tooty-pooty-splew
The hippos are going to nibble you!

Even worse than this, Capitán Fantástico was staring at the wooden wall of the barn and it was starting to smoulder!

"You are not the real Alfonso Aparador! And your make-up advice is rubbish!" yelled Ginalolobrigida.

This made Alfonso begin reciting even more loudly:

Your bottom is so wide and fat,
Your face looks like a bird poo splat,
You think you're pretty but you're wrong -
You're ugly and you really pong!

This was the nastiest and rudest thing that Ginalolobrigida had ever heard. "I hate you, fake Alfonso!" she growled.

By now part of the barn wall was on fire

and another part of the wall had almost been bitten through by the mechanical mini hippos. *EMERGENCIA!*

But what was Brian doing while all of this was happening?

Well, Brian was trying to enjoy getting carried about by some of the other Brian Llamas and being called king by the hundreds of llamas following him. He couldn't really enjoy it, though. It all seemed silly. He didn't feel very much like a king. He just wanted to be an ordinary llama and have fun with his friends.

"Brians, please just take me to my barn. I would like a lie down."

"WHO SHOULD WE DESTROY WHILE WE MARCH TO YOUR BARN, KING BRIAN?"

"No, no. Please and thank you, just take me home." The purple-eyed Brians were scaring poor Brian.

"YES! WE WILL OBEY YOUR ORDERS! THEN WE WILL DESTORY EVERYONE AND CONQUER FIRST SCOTLANDANDTHENTHEWORLD!"

Of course, this made all of Brian's fur stand up in fright, so that he looked like a chocolate candyfloss explosion with frightened eyes. "Dear other Señor Brians, please do not. Gracias."

Brian only got more frightened when he turned the corner and saw his barn being attacked on all sides, with mini hippos eating it, Alfonso yelling horrible poems and Capitán Fantástico setting bits of it on fire.

"Oh, no! EMERGENCIA!" Brian yelled.

Hearing Brian, Carlos called out, "Is that King Brian?"

"It is just me, Brian. I do not want to be a king," Brian shouted back. And then he had an idea. "Brians?"

"YES!"

"Am I your king?" he asked.

"YES!"

"Oh, there he goes being better than everyone else," shouted Guinevere from inside the burning and eaten-away barn.

"Help us you foolish fool!" shouted Ginalolobrigida.

Brian tried to sound kingly. "Please, Brians, obey me and fight those wicked and strange creatures attacking my barn. Please. But do not hurt them too much, thank you!"

The purple-eyed Brians carrying Brian and following him in a crowd didn't answer. Their

223

eyes began to shine brighter and brighter. Then the llamas carrying him all kicked and jumped until he fell to the ground. Slowly, they began to surround him, staring and staring at him horribly until his fur got hotter and hotter and began to singe.

Oh, what will our llama pals do? How will they escape?

EMERGENCIA! 🐾

WONDERFUL SEWER RATS

SECTION TWENTY-THREE

In which there are two especially wonderful

sewer rats. And an especially wonderful

thing. And an especially wonderful uncle!

In Sylvester Pearlyclaws' Supervillain Lair, everything was as smelly and horrible as usual and a little bit more evil than ever before.

This was because Pearlyclaws was working all his controls (with his hands and feet at once) to make his mechanical creatures on the llama farm frighten our llama chums. He was hoping that before long they would all be eaten up by the clickety metal jaws of his nasty machine animals.

He was busy enjoying himself and tickling his purplonium and turning his remote control dials and dancing dreadful dances of evil with his floppy feet. He was enjoying his cruelness so much that he stopped whispering evil things along the Purple Internet. He was enjoying waggling his nasty hands and hooting his nasty hoots of joy so much that he didn't check his monitors.

That meant he didn't see what happened when Uncle Shawn and all our friends held hands under the sea and sent a great big thought back through the rainbow-shining wool and into the Purple Internet!

Uncle Shawn, Bill, Sky, Sam, Timothy and Florence all thought together after three – ONE, TWO, THREE – *"BE NICER! BE KINDER! BE EVEN KINDER THAN THAT!"*

And for a few seconds all of Pearlyclaws' monitors showed Uncle Shawn's face, looking as happy and kind and helpful as anyone can.

As you will remember, Bernard and Katie Pinktail the sewer rats worked for Pearlyclaws in his lair. He had promised them all kinds of wonderful presents – a camembert mountain, disco boots, a time machine; all the things that rats love. But he had never even paid them with a small slice of mouldy cheddar. And he had pulled their tails and called them names and been nasty to them.

ALL THE THINGS RATS LOVE

1. CAMEMBERT MOUNTAIN

2. DISCO BOOTS

3. A TIME MACHINE

Of course, when the Pinktails looked up at the monitors, they saw Uncle Shawn smiling and waving and felt a big wave of kindness and cosiness rush through all their fur.

All at once they understood this was THE UNCLE SHAWN – the uncle who always helps any creatures who are in trouble, no matter what. Oh, no! They had been helping Pearlyclaws harm THAT UNCLE SHAWN!

The Pinktails knew they had to stop working for Pearlyclaws at once. They didn't feel a little bit bad about running off to help Uncle Shawn.

Pearlyclaws was about to learn that if you are nasty to people and animals they may not want to help you when you need help.

And so, while Pearlyclaws was dancing and chuckling chuckles that sounded like sad toads falling into holes, the Pinktails were happily scampering from valve to valve and pushing the levers that opened watertight doors. And the doors were the only things that stopped the River Thames sweeping into the lair and washing it all away!

Pearlyclaws thought it was just about time to flip the switch that would mean all his mechanical monsters would destroy Brian and all the llamas and the llama farm. He turned to look at the monitors, while Bernard and Katie were hopping neatly into their tiny canoe and then...

They both pulled down the final lever – the one that let all the sewer water come pouring into the sewer pipe. Pearlyclaws only had time to glance at his monitors and say, "Isn't that—?" before – SPLEAUSSSHHH – in rushed the river and sewer water.

FLOOD LAIR WITH SEWAGE

TURN ON LIGHTS

TURN ON HEATING

As Katie and Bernard's canoe surfed along on the waves, out into the Thames, horrible smelly water swept through the whole of Pearlyclaws' lair.

Pearlyclaws' one big leather chair (with threatening arms) tumbled out into the Thames (where little fish would eventually play in it and plants would grow on its seat). His Dungeon of Despair filled with dirty water. His Bedroom of Nastiness also filled with sewer water. And his Bathroom of Horror and his Kitchenette of Wickedness got even wetter and more horrible. His toast was ruined. And his big jar of purplonium fell down and down and stuck in the mud of the riverbed.

And Pearlyclaws himself? He was swept away out into the Thames as well and so – *ffeeep ffeeep* – was his false nose. Eventually a conger eel found the false nose and wore it as a jaunty hat when he held parties.

The Pinktails' canoe rushed along the river until it deposited them on a lovely soft mud bank.

Then they danced together – a scampery, pink-tailed dance that celebrated the end of Sylvester Pearlyclaws. There was a lot of tail waving.

The Pinktails went to live in Ipswich and never worked for any supervillains ever again. In fact, they opened a small dance studio, which was very successful. That was the end of their time with Pearlyclaws.

But was that really the end of Pearlyclaws..?

Hmmm…

Well… 🐾

TERRIFIED LLAMAS

SECTION TWENTY-FOUR

*In which there is a lot more height
than the llamas expect...*

Meanwhile, on Uncle Shawn's llama farm it seemed that Guinevere and Carlos and Ginalolobrigida were going to be munched and crunched by metal jaws or scorched and scrooched by purple fire inside Brian's barn! Or both! And outside the barn Brian was surrounded by evil purple-eyed Brians who were trying to scorch and scrooch him and maybe there would be munching soon after that!

But just when everyone had closed their eyes and held their breath and nearly lost hope...

While Brian held his breath, all those good kind thoughts from Uncle Shawn and our friends rushed along the Purple Internet. They whooshed and swooshed like a river cleaning out a sewer pipe, only they were even bigger and started to shine and sparkle with rainbow colours.

While Guinevere held her breath, different bits of purplonium were talking to each other and deciding to be nice and part of the Living Fish Tree magic. Ripples of rainbow light were spreading further and further, faster than Florence the shark, all through every bit of purplonium on Earth.

While Carlos and Ginalolobrigida held their breath, the purple clouds, the purple stains in the lakes and rivers, and even Pearlyclaws' jar of purple purplonium had changed colour and started to shine with friendliness.

And then all our friends heard strange, deafening sounds – *TWUNG! SPLAGANG! SPOINGYOING!* It sounded like tons of evil scaffolding landing on top of a heap of horrible lawnmowers which were balancing on a stack of terrible alarm clocks.

Everyone jumped, worried they were hearing some new horrible monster.

"Oooohhh. I am most muchly afraid," whispered Brian. But then – because he was also very brave – Brian opened one eye. And then the other eye. And then he saw...

All of the purple-eyed Brians had collapsed in heaps of cogs and wheels and springs and fake fur.

The wicked wiggly hippos, the fake llama superhero and the terrible mechanical llama poet had also fallen into messy heaps.

And a tangle of mechanical spider legs and dull, extinguished eyes tumbled from the rafters of the barn and smashed into pieces, which allowed Claude to swing free on his thread and yell, "Hooray!"

Of course, no one could hear him.

Ginalolobrigida sighed loudly inside the barn. "Now what have you done, you foolish King Brian?"

"Please and thank you I think that everything is going to be very fine," said Brian, grinning and clicking his hooves, but then...

Very strange things started to happen.

Everywhere the purplonium had once been, making creatures feel grumpy and sad, all the fishes and people and animals started to feel well and happy. In offices and buses and in houses and tents and in tower blocks and cottages, in submarines and ships, in football grounds and schools, everyone started to smile. Rainbow flickers of light floated by in the clouds and slipped about under the water, or flowed across birds' wings as they flew.

This was because, dancing around the Living Fish Tree, all of our friends were still thinking as hard as they could – and then a little bit harder than that – *"BE KIND. BE KINDER. BE HAPPY. BE FREE."*

And further off in the ocean a huge ring of Extremely Great White Sharks were dancing and twisting and turning around the Living Fish Tree and humming, "MMM-mmm-MMM-mmm", the song of happy sharks. Slowly, patches and stripes of rainbow light were covering the sharks' sides and backs and tummies until they shone like magic happening. Because magic was happening!

"It's working!" shouted Uncle Shawn and smiled his biggest ever smile. "All over the world the purplonium has turned into Living Fish Tree magic and now it's coming home!"

And as he spoke more and more rainbow twists and balls and whooshes of rainbow light were gathering and covering the Living Fish Tree with wonder.

But even Uncle Shawn didn't suspect that back at the llama farm there was so much purplonium turning into Living Fish Tree magic that soon the whole barn and the ground under it and around it had begun to glow brighter and brighter, and then slowly tear away and lift up into the air.

Our llama friends – and Claude – had no time to say, "WHHHOAOAH!" They were flying as fast as thinking, all the way to the Pacific and the Living Fish Tree!

And if everyone else hadn't been so busy feeling wonderful and dancing and shining with colours,

they might have noticed a barn and a bit of field flying overhead. But nobody did see anything.

"WAAAAAAAAAAAAAAAAAAAAA!!!! EMERGENCIAAAAAAAAAAAAAAA!!!!!" yelled Brian, as the ground whisked past and the high altitude breezes tickled his ears.

"What is it now?" asked Carlos from inside the barn.

"Please and thank you, perhaps open the barn door and look. We are flying!"

Ginalolobrigida grumbled, "Oh, Brian you are such an idiot." But when she and the other llamas had managed to open the door they did indeed see the clouds pelting by and the ground far below.

"Oooohhh," they all said.

"I am sorry I was being king for a while. I did not like it. You are my real llama friends. The other Brians were bad Brians," whispered Brian. And as he felt a tickle on his ear, he said, "Ah, hello my friend Señor Claude. I have missed you. It is much better to be guarded by one wonderful tiny spider than by hundreds of nasty llamas."

"I love you," said Claude in his tiny voice, waving four of his legs with joy.

Carlos said, "You tried to save us, Brian. We know you're our friend. And you really are brave."

"Yes," agreed Guinevere, and nuzzled Brian's nose.

Ginalolobrigida said, "Please everyone, lick

off my horrible eyeshadow. If I am going to be on a flying island I want to look my best. Then I will forget all about that terrible Alfonso who was not as good and nice and kind as the llamas I already know."

And so – rather bouncily, because they were in a barn on a flying lump of Scotland – Carlos and Guinevere and Brian licked off Ginalolobrigida's make-up. It didn't taste wonderful, but they wanted her to feel happier.

They were just beginning to enjoy their wonderful flight and the lovely views, when the barn and the land sank lower and lower across the Pacific Ocean.

Carlos was just about to say, "Well, this is even more fun," when – **SPLABOOSH** – the whole shed landed in the Pacific and began – oh no! – to sink down into the depths.

EMERGENCIA!!!!

But the new bits of magic had brought the llamas straight to the Living Fish Tree, the home of Living Fish Tree magic. So the wide-awake and well and glowing giant octopus caught the little bit of Uncle Shawn's farm and the barn gently in her arms and set it carefully down on the ocean floor.

Sam and Sky and Bill and Uncle Shawn and all the sharks were still dancing as hard as they could and hadn't at all expected to see Brian's barn and a bit of meadow suddenly underwater with them.

BARN FISH

"OOoh!" cried Bill. "That fish looks exactly like Brian's barn. Is there a barn fish?"

"Quick!" shouted Uncle Shawn. "It *is* Brian's barn! And look! There's Brian!"

Brian was indeed floating about upside down and trying to hold his breath, but his eyes were very big and scared. Llamas don't belong underwater.

Uncle Shawn knew just what to do. He rushed in on his long legs and fed a big, long handful of powdered air to Brian and asked, "Sam, please pull the barn door open! Sky, throw in some of your powdered air! I think more of our friends are in trouble!"

The twins ran forward and saved the llamas, who were very surprised and wet and close to drowning. Soon the barn was full of powdered air and rainbow lights and Bill and Uncle Shawn and Sky and Sam and all the llamas and everyone could hug everyone else (while Claude ran across their heads and patted them with his feet and yelled, "WOO! WEE!" at the top of his voice).

"But why are there lots of bent and broken bits of machinery next to the barn on this bit of meadow?" asked Sky. "And lots of furry shapes that look like llamas?"

"And why do most of the llamas look like Brian – only nasty?" asked Sam.

"Never mind that," said Bill. "Why is there a bit of Scotland here at the bottom of the Pacific?"

Uncle Shawn laughed. "Hooray! This means the Living Fish Tree is cured! Well done everyone! Our thinking and dancing turned all the purplonium into Living Fish Tree magic. Everything here must have been covered in especially bad purplonium and so it is covered in especially good magic now. The Living Fish Tree was strong enough to call it home with all the rest of the magic." Uncle Shawn held out some more powdered air to Claude and the llamas. "Here, munch some of this and come outside."

And so Brian slowly led the three other llamas out of the barn and they were all able to see the wonderful rainbow-sparkling Living Fish Tree

AN UNDERSEA WONDERLAND OF LOVE AND HAPPINESS

and feel her limb tips stroke their ears and look into her wonderfully wise eyes. And they could stare at the sea mountains and the watery light and the brightly coloured fish and—

"WAAAAAAAAAAAAAAAAAAAA!!!!!!! EMERGENCIA!!!!!!!!!!!!"

Carlos and Guinevere and Ginalolobrigida all noticed the vast number of sharks who were circling and dancing shark dances in the distance. And the two Extremely Great White Sharks, Timothy and Florence, who were right there, grinning at them in a terrifying way!

But what did Brian do? Brian, who had been so scared he had dreamed up an army of Brians to protect him: what did he do?

He took a deep breath. Then he jammed his left back knee against his right back knee. Then he held his left front knee tight against his right front knee – so that none of them would tremble. Then he looked carefully at how happy and peaceful the sharks seemed. And he saw how beautifully they were dancing and heard their song. And then he caught the eye of Timothy the shark, who had never ever seen a llama before and was desperate to nuzzle one and speak to one and maybe play with him. Timothy had such sparkly and friendly eyes that Brian said, in a very brave voice, "Hola, Señor Tiburón."

"Ooh, ooh, ooh," said Timothy, trying to wag his tail as softly as possible. "Is that *Hello, Mister Shark* in llama language?"

"It is, Mister Shark."

"I'm Timothy. Let's play! Please, please Mum, can I play with the llama?"

"If you're careful." Florence nodded.

Brian smiled at Uncle Shawn and the others. "I am going to play with this gigantunormous and horrifying shark, Uncle Shawn. I think I am feeling brave today. Or maybe I have been so scared that I have no more scaredness left."

Everyone was very impressed.

Uncle Shawn stroked Brian's woolly neck. "Of course you can play, but don't go too far. We will have to go home soon. And be careful – some of those sharks might be scared of llamas." He winked.

While Brian rolled head over heels with Timothy and rode on his nose and generally had lots of fun, Carlos and Guinevere and Ginalolobrigida told Bill and Uncle Shawn about all the horrible excitement that had been going on back at the llama farm.

And while they did that, Claude the spider bounced about inside a big bubble of air and waved his arms and legs at the sea creatures.

Sam and Sky were looking at the bits of broken clockwork. "I wonder what will happen to all this mess?"

Bill asked Uncle Shawn, "Do you think we can do something with them?"

Uncle Shawn leaned in and listened while the Living Fish Tree whispered to him. Then Uncle Shawn said, "I think she has plans to mend them with her magic and make them useful."

Bill said, "She could turn them into cleaning machines for the oceans and rivers and lakes and seas. And they could be rescuing machines, too – in case anything got into trouble in the water. Would that be good?"

Uncle Shawn hugged his best friend. "Then they could use everything they cleaned up to make more cleaning machines until everywhere was clean and safe!"

"Yes! And sometimes they could just swim about for fun!"

RESCUING MACHINE

CLEANING MACHINE

SWIMMING-ABOUT-FOR-FUN MACHINE

Brian swam back from playing with Timothy and then Uncle Shawn and Bill and Sam and Sky and all the llamas hugged the Living Fish Tree goodbye, knowing that they had nearly reached their happy ending and hoping the sea creatures could reach theirs, too.

It was time for everyone to climb into the barn full of powdered air on top of the lump of Scotland and go home.

Timothy the shark was sad that all his new friends were leaving, but he promised to visit them when he was next passing Shoogeldy Bay.

"I won't cry. I'm not crying," he said in his quietest voice – the one which only rattled all the planks in the barn. Even though this was a fib, no purple cloud appeared anywhere near his bottom.

NOT CRYING

Everyone pretended they couldn't see Timothy the soft-hearted shark crying. "You're a big brave shark. And we're not crying, either." Then they all hugged him.

And, even though they were telling kind fibs, nobody's bottom produced a big purple cloud. The Living Fish Tree really was doing her magical work again!

Then the world's largest and wisest and most magical octopus smiled, winked and used a special *whhooooosh* of magic to lift the barn up out of the ocean and then fly it, faster than you can burn a pancake, or hug a friend, or eat a scone, all the way back to Uncle Shawn's farm where it landed and fitted right back into place.

And I'm sure that's the end of all the excitement, aren't you?

Well... 🐾

SECTION TWENTY-FIVE

In which – oh dearie, dearie me! – maybe there is more excitement. This section also contains puddings.

Finally, it was Pandrumdroochit Pudding Day. There were no more purple bottom explosions and no purpleness left in the sky. After having so many adventures, all our friends were enjoying the celebrations.

RICE
PUDDING

Claude was running backwards across a bowl of rice pudding that had been put out for him in Brian's barn. The barn was just the way it had always been – only a little bit more salty.

Carlos and Guinevere Llama were looking forward to the Long Distance Pudding Throwing Competition. They had been practising catching puddings in their mouths for weeks.

Ginalolobrigida Llama was teaching the pudding chefs of Pandrumdroochit how to colour their puddings so that they would always be stylish – even if they were eating custard with their hands, because of being very hungry.

Brian was asking people he had never met before to buy raffle tickets, which was really brave of him. He didn't even think about counting his hooves to see if they had been stolen.

Meanwhile, Bill and Uncle Shawn were strolling along beneath the cliffs at the north end of Shoogeldy Bay and eating sea-salted toffee ice-cream puddings. Delicious!

Bill wiped ice cream from his long nose. "Uncle Shawn? Won't it be hard to tell when people are lying now?"

"Yes, people can tell lies now, without losing their pants. That's why it's always important to check what people do, as well as what they say. If they do bad things, maybe you should check they aren't telling bad lies, too." Uncle Shawn smiled at Bill. "But aren't you Badger Bill, the shark-riding adventurer?"

Bill blushed and adjusted his pirate hat. He had started wearing it again, now that everyone could lie and say it suited him. "Well, I'm not famous enough to be on a quilt..." His tail and ears wiggled in pleasure – and Uncle Shawn's hair wiggled back.

"No other badger has ever met the Living Fish Tree. Or flown in a barn. I have written to the Big Badger Supply Company and told them you should be on their Famous Badger Explorer quilts. And I sent them a drawing of you in Timothy's mouth." Uncle Shawn scratched his head. "I hope that doesn't make them think you got eaten..."

Bill and Uncle Shawn were walking to watch the Fly a Pudding Kite Competition. No one ever could get their pudding to fly like a kite, but it was still fun. The Pudding Launch Area was up on the cliffs and so it was easy to wait on the beach below and just open your mouth to eat the puddings as they fell.

PUDDING KITES OF THE WORLD

THE FLATTENED FLAN
(failed to become airborne)

CUSTARD SKIN BOX KITE
(flew out to sea, not seen again. Possibly carried by seagull)

SEMOLINA SPITFIRE
(biscuit supports fell apart in flight, flattened owner)

RICE PUDDING KITTYHAWK
(dropped like a stone)

FAR FLUNG JELLY
(flung - 76cm, flown - 0cm)

PUFF PASTRY FRISBEE
WITH LEMON CURD
(fell 2 metres, bounced 5 metres)

CHRISTMAS PUDDING ROCKET
(disqualified)

JUMPING JUNKET
(flew 3 metres)

STEAMED PUDDING SOARER
(maximum height soared - 27cm)

As the best friends strolled, a strange shape flew above them. It didn't look much like a pudding – or much like a kite. And it was making a funny *ffeeep, ffeeep* noise, almost like a very evil person's Number Four Emergency Replacement Nose...

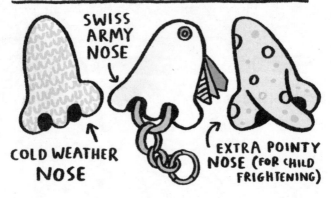

EMERGENCY REPLACEMENT NOSES

SWISS ARMY NOSE

COLD WEATHER NOSE

EXTRA POINTY NOSE (FOR CHILD FRIGHTENING)

"Hmmm..." said Uncle Shawn, looking up into the sky. "That's flying very well for a pudding. I didn't think the competition had started."

"Ooh-uggh-ech," coughed Bill. "What is that horrible smell? It's like stinky poo."

And do we know who might smell like stinky poo? And who makes *ffeeep, ffeeep* noises? Maybe someone who was the wickedest human on Earth?

Oh, yes!

Oh, no!

It was Sylvester Wilberforce Humbertly Pearlyclaws!

Pearlyclaws had swum all the way from London, using his flippery feet. (And even all that water hadn't washed away the stink of his sewer pipe lair.)

He had reached Shoogeldy Bay the night before, crept up out of the sea and flappety-flopped his way up onto dry land. There he had seen the noticeboards that were set out ready for Pandrumdroochit Pudding Day, telling everybody the day's events. There he read about the Fly a Pudding Kite Competition.

This gave him a horrible idea. Pearlyclaws collected some sticks and then used them to stretch out his flat, flat feet further than they had ever gone. Pearlyclaws had turned his whole wicked self into a wicked kite!

And now, up in the sky above Bill and Uncle Shawn, his tender feet were in stinging, stretched agony. "Naaaaaaaaaaa!" Pearlyclaws screamed with fear of heights and foot pain and hatred. "This time I'll get you! This time you'll be got!" He sped through the air towards our chums. "What did you do to my purplonium!?! I'll grab you both up and then drop you on the pointy rocks!"

While Bill stared in horror, Pearlyclaws swooped nearer, reaching his hands out, like the gripping claws of a mighty bird of prey – only much smellier.

"Are you sure you want to do this?" Uncle Shawn shouted, holding Bill's hand.

"I'll look after you, Uncle Shawn," whispered Bill in a shaky voice.

"Sylvester. You have one last chance not to do this terrible thing!" called Uncle Shawn, his blue eyes shining.

But Pearlyclaws kept zooming towards them. Now they could see his cruel eyes and his cruel nose: *ffeeep – ffeeep*.

Bill was really worried.

But then…

Uncle Shawn looked out to sea and started laughing.

And then...

Uncle Shawn started dancing.

"No, no! Get down!" shouted Bill as Pearlyclaws rushed even nearer to Uncle Shawn, his nose noise speeding – *ffeeepffeeepffeeepffeeepffeeepffeeepffeeepffeeepffeeep...*

But then...

HOORAY!

Sweeping up out of the sea like a shark-shaped rocket came Timothy the wonderful and friendly shark. His sides shone with sparkling Living Fish Tree magic.

Clever Uncle Shawn had noticed Timothy's fin in the water, just in time to dance his Quick Help Us Dance.

Bill and Uncle Shawn had enough time to say, "Ooh!"

Then Timothy's razor sharp teeth whooshed

past Pearlyclaws and made him yell, "EEEK!!!"

But Timothy didn't want to eat something as nasty as Pearlyclaws. He just used his massive tail to swipe Pearlyclaws over two fields, three hedges, a bicycle and a tea tent.

Then the wickedest man in the world landed in Pandrumdroochit's world-record-breaking vat of mango pudding.

SMACK!

WICKEDEST MAN IN THE WORLD

MANGO PUDDING

Pearlyclaws went straight to the bottom and Mrs Wallace only noticed he was there when she found a false nose in her helping of pudding. Then she saw a furious bald head emerge from the vat, all sticky and unhappy. "I hate mango! I hate you, stupid woman! I hate everyone!"

It took four hours for all of Pandrumdroochit's firefighters and seventeen police officers to pull Pearlyclaws from the sticky pudding, while he yelled, "I'll get you, Uncle Shawn! Next time, I'll get you!"

They had to wash him down with hoses before they could handcuff him and take him away.

Uncle Shawn and Bill didn't watch. They walked out into the shallow water and thanked Timothy for being so clever and leaping so high and tickled his sides. Then they promised to write a waterproof postcard to tell his mum about how wonderful he had been.

They could just about hear Pearlyclaws yelling in the distance, "I hate you! I hate you all!"

Uncle Shawn just shook his head.

Timothy said, "If he is nasty to you again I will swim up and find him and nibble off all of his edges until he is round like a biscuit." Then he winked at Uncle Shawn and Bill so that they knew he probably didn't mean it.

And after so much excitement, everyone came down to the beach and watched the pudding kites not flying and tried to eat as much falling pudding as they could. And Uncle Shawn swam out to give Timothy a big bowl of custard, which he really liked – mainly because it had sardines in it.

That night Carlos and Guinevere slept like llamas who are full of pudding and whose dreams are full of sparkling light – dreams that are going to stay exactly where they should.

And Ginalolobrigida Llama dreamed that she was flying with gorgeous birds and completely ignoring Alfonso Aparador as she swept past him, beautifully.

And Brian snuggled into his straw bed, feeling much braver than he ever had before. He called up to Claude the spider, "Good night

Señor Claude. I will defend you if anyone comes to disturb your web."

And Claude called back, "And I will defend you if anyone comes to disturb your fur. Good night."

And the two friends went to sleep and had dreams full of bubbles and shark grins and fun.

And Uncle Shawn and Badger Bill sat on the veranda drinking cocoa and watched the sun setting. Bill was sitting in his badger-sized rocking chair and Uncle Shawn was sitting in his Uncle Shawn-sized

rocking chair. They felt a little bit tired, but very happy. They liked adventures, but they liked cocoa and hugs and sunsets and peacefulness, too.

"What's black and white and makes a lot of noise?" asked Bill.

"A zebra with a trumpet." Uncle Shawn smiled. "And what's a porcupine's favourite food?"

"Prickled onions."

"Of course! You are very clever, Explorer Bill!"

Then they sat together and told more jokes until they were both sleepy.

"Well," said Uncle Shawn, "that was quite an adventure. It was fun, but tomorrow, I hope we just make toast and read books." He patted Bill's arm. "Thank you for being my friend. I love you, Bill."

"And I love you, Uncle Shawn."

"Time to have some dreams."

"Yes." Bill stood up and grinned. "And we'll only make the nice ones come true." 🐾

A. L. KENNEDY

A. L. Kennedy was born in a small Scottish town far too long ago and has written books for adults and children, but mainly adults. Before that she made up stories to amuse herself. It has always surprised her that her job involves doing one of the things she loves most and she's very grateful to be a writer. She has won awards for her books in several countries. She has travelled all over the world and enjoyed it immensely. She plays the banjo badly, but makes up for this by never playing it anywhere near anyone else.

GEMMA CORRELL

Gemma Correll is a cartoonist, writer, illustrator and all-round small person. She is the author of *A Pug's Guide to Etiquette* and *Doodling for Dog People*, and the illustrator of *Pig and Pug* by Lynne Berry, *Being a Girl* by Hayley Long and *The Trials of Ruby P. Baxter* by Joanna Nadin (among other things). Her illustrations look like a five-year-old drew them because she hires one to do all her work for her. She pays him in fudge. His name is Alan.